VAMPIRE VIGILANTES

THERE'S TOO MUCH AT STAKE...

Book One

INVASION OF THE SAUSAGE SNATCHERS

Written by
Michael Cox

Illustrated by
Chris Smedley

Hodder
Children's
Books

a division of Hodder Headline Limited

The Eck Valley Region

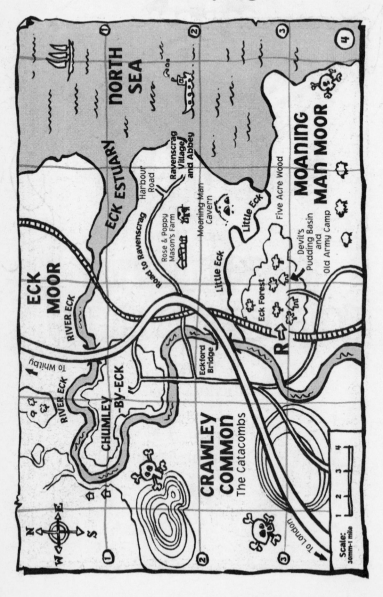

Chumley Town Map

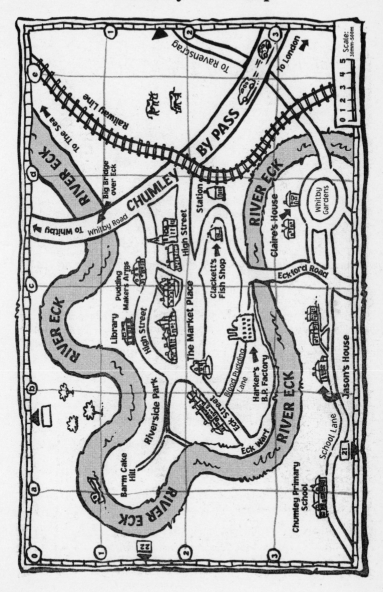

To Jo and Tom – M.C.

Text copyright © 2002 Michael Cox
Illustrations copyright © 2002 Chris Smedley

First published in Great Britain in 2002
by Hodder Children's Books

10 9 8 7 6 5 4 3 2 1

A Catalogue record for this book is available from the British Library

ISBN 0 340 79592 1

Printed and bound in Great Britain by
Guernsey Press Ltd, Guernsey, Channel Islands

Hodder Children's Books
A division of Hodder Headline Limited
338 Euston Road, London NW1 3BH

Chapter One
The Blodvats

When the whole thing was finally over, Claire knew she wouldn't have missed even one second of it for anything. But while it was actually happening there were quite a few times she definitely wished it wasn't!

It all began after her mum and dad got back from their mega-posh wine tasting holiday in France. They'd come home full of stories of vineyards and villas and dreary stuff like that. None of which was the slightest bit exciting for a computer crazy ten-year-old like Claire. The more she listened, the more glad she felt she'd given the French bore-tour a miss and stayed at home in Chumley-by-Eck with Grandpa Reg and Wendy.

But she was really pleased for her mum and dad because they'd had such a great time and had made friends with this really nice couple at their hotel, called the Blodvats. Mr and Mrs Whimsy had hit it off with them from the word go. Each evening they'd meet in the hotel restaurant and the four of them would pass the time chatting. Apparently, the Blodvats were filthy rich and lived in a castle in Tonsilveinia, and had a huge cellar full of bottles of really old red wine, which they called Peasants' Blood – but only for a joke, ha ha!

They also had a handsome son called Vladimir, who was in Germany studying to be a concert pianist, and three lovely daughters who were away at boarding school in Switzerland. At the end of the hol, Mr and Mrs Whimsy and the Blodvats had swapped addresses and said, 'If you're ever in our neck of the woods, pop in and say hello!' like lots of people do – but then forget about it a few days afterwards.

About three months later, one stormy September's evening, Claire had gone to see her friend, Jason Turner, to check out his new PC. When she arrived home a few hours afterwards she got a bit of a shock. Parked in the front drive was the most enormous black Mercedes estate car. It was so big it made her mum and dad's car look like a toy. Her first thought was that someone had died and no one had bothered to tell her, because the monstrous car looked just like an undertaker's hearse. She felt quite worried until her mum came to the door, looking all excited.

'Claire, the Blodvats are here!' she gasped, as if royalty had come to visit.

'The Blod who?' said Claire.

'The Blodvats!' said her mum. 'The couple we met on holiday. Come and say hello!' And she shepherded Claire in to meet the guests of honour.

Dr Bruno Blodvat and his wife, Hildegard, were sitting on the settee in the front room, chatting to Dad and Grandpa Reg. They were the oddest-looking couple Claire had ever seen.

Mrs Blodvat was as skinny as spaghetti and really tiny, with a narrow, pointy face that made her look like an extremely shifty miniature whippet. She had long, thin lips, glittery, green eyes and her skin was as pale as egg white, as if she never went out of doors. Which was odd because she was dressed from head to toe in hiking gear: walking boots as big as buckets, purple corduroy trousers, a fleecy pink jacket, and a bright yellow bobble hat, which didn't go at all well with her long, dangly, death's head earrings.

Dr Bruno Blodvat, who was also togged

up in outdoor clobber, was enormous. He must have been at least six feet six and was as wide as a wardrobe. The expression on his big pasty face immediately made Claire think of those smarmy TV-show hosts who keep their totally unpleasant personalities hidden behind sickly false smiles.

The moment Claire walked into the room, Dr Bruno leapt off the settee and clicked his heels together so sharply they made a sound like a gun going off, then he bowed so low that his huge beaky nose almost touched the carpet. After that he reached out and took her hand in his. And that was when she noticed that the tips of his fingers were missing. He lifted her hand to his mouth and kissed it. She felt as if someone had stuck an ice lolly on her knuckles. His lips were freezing.

Mrs Blodvat simply gave Claire a cool smile, then rested her long, black-painted fingernails on her shoulder, and said, 'Pleased to meet you, my dear. Oh, what pretty liddle ears you heff. And what a loffely, long, slim neck.' Claire felt like she'd just been spoken to by a puff adder.

'Actually, Claire,' said her mum. 'Hildegard was just showing us some snaps of Vladimir and the girls.'

'Yes, yes!' cried Hildegard. 'And you must

see them too!' Then she began bombarding Claire with the photos.

The Blodvats' children were very attractive. Vladimir was small and studious-looking with gold-rimmed spectacles, gentle blue eyes, soft brown curls, a golden tan and an utterly charming, shy smile. He was dressed in a bow tie and tails and was sitting at a grand piano. The girls were petite, blonde and blue-eyed. All three were wearing pastel-coloured party frocks and were smiling angelically.

Claire didn't know quite what to say. If she'd been honest she might have said, 'How ever did a couple of face-aches like you two manage to produce such great looking kids?' but that wouldn't have been good manners, so she just handed back the pictures and said, 'Hmmm, very nice . . . er, thanks very much.'

'Dr Bruno and Hildegard are staying at a bed and breakfast quite near to us, Claire,' her dad chipped in. 'They're over here doing research work for Sir Norman Goreman, the British Minister for Tourism. It's very hush hush!'

'Zat is right!' said Hildegard, tapping her nose and fixing Claire with her green, staring eyes. 'But now ve are heffing a little holiday in your loffely Yorkshire. Seeing your sights. Ve are most interested in your hysterical old buildings.'

'And your famous peoples,' said Dr Bruno. 'Perhaps ve vill be bumping into Sir Robin Hood or liddle Oliver Twist?'

None of the Whimsys knew quite what to make of this because although it sounded like a joke, Bruno had said it with a completely straight face. So Mrs Whimsy quickly said, 'And you're fascinated by our local customs and crafts, aren't you?'

'Oh, ve certainly are!' said Dr Bruno. 'Grandpa Vej here has been telling us that he is the most famous bloody sausage maker in all off Yorkshirepuddingland!'

'Ectually,' interrupted Mrs Blodvat, giving Dr Bruno the sort of smile that strips paint from walls, 'I sink zat you mean blood pudding maker, my dear.'

'Well yer both wrong!' piped up Grandpa Reg. "Cos round 'ere we mostly call 'em black puddings. Although of course they are made from blood – pigs' blood, that is! Now! The most fascinating thing about a black pudding . . .'

And with that, Grandpa Reg launched into one of his 'black puddings are the most interesting subject on Earth' marathons, while the Blodvats leaned forward, smiling and nodding, saying things like, 'Is zat so?' and 'Vell I never!'. They really did appear to be genuinely interested. Which surprised

Claire, because most people's reaction to his puddingathons was either to fall asleep or suddenly remember they had an urgent space shuttle to catch.

Once Grandpa Reg got on the black pudding trail he could keep going for weeks, so Claire excused herself and went to help her mum prepare tea. She also wanted to ask where Wendy was. Normally he was the friendliest of dogs and whenever they had guests he'd be leaping all over them with his tail waggling around like the Queen's hand at a garden party.

'Mum,' said Claire, as she buttered a slice of bread. 'Where's Wendy?'

Mrs Whimsy suddenly looked serious, then said, 'Err, we've had a bit of a problem with Wendy . . .'

'What sort of a problem?' exclaimed Claire.

'He's been naughty,' said Mrs Whimsy. 'Not only did he growl at Bruno and Hildegard the moment they got here but he also did you know what.'

'You mean he—?'

'Yes – exactly!' said Mrs Whimsy.

Claire thought she'd noticed a rather unpleasant smell in the front room. Although Wendy was a nice dog, he did have this habit of making bad smells whenever he got excited or upset. Which is why, of course, they called him Wendy!

'The odd thing is, he started acting strangely before they arrived,' said Mrs Whimsy. 'And we weren't even expecting them.'

'How weird!' said Claire. 'So where's Wendy now?'

'Hiding in the garage,' said Mrs Whimsy. 'He ran out there after he'd disgraced himself.'

'I'll just go and say hello,' said Claire.

She found Wendy cowering in the garage. As usual, he was really pleased to see her and raced around wagging his tail like they'd been separated for years. But when she tried to get him to come in and make friends with the Blodvats he backed into a corner, whimpering and trembling like a leaf. Even when Claire tried to bribe him with his favourite dog biscuits he refused to budge, so in the end she said, 'Suit yourself, soppy old thing!' and went back to help her mum.

As she was crossing the drive Claire glanced into the Blodvats' car and saw something that made her jump. Leering up at her from the front seat was a picture of a skull on the cover of a battered and ancient looking book. Next to the book lay a large road atlas, open at a map of Yorkshire. By the light from the porch lamp Claire could just make out that someone had drawn lots of tiny skulls at various points around the map then joined them to a letter 'R' with dotted lines. But the car's interior was so gloomy she couldn't tell exactly where the 'R' was, although it looked like it might be quite near Chumley.

All this for a holiday? thought Claire. Some people have strange ideas of fun! Whatever sort of fun activities the Blodvats were planning they'd certainly brought plenty of clothes. The back of their gigantic car was crammed with luggage. Well, Claire assumed it was luggage. It was hard to tell as most of it was hidden under a large black velvet cloth. And, if those shapes were luggage, they certainly made their suitcases big in Tonsilveinia. Some of them seemed to be the size of fridge freezers. Probably big enough to fit Mrs Blodvat in, not to mention her giant hiking boots, thought Claire with a smile.

As well as the luggage, there were two enormous sacks. One of them had a small tear in it and Claire could just make out something brown and crumbly, like instant coffee granules, that had trickled from the hole. Just as she was wondering why on earth anyone would take sacks of coffee on holiday, a cold finger of fear brushed the nape of her neck and she got the uncanny feeling she was being watched.

She turned and saw Hildegard staring at her from the front room window. It wasn't a very friendly stare. For some reason she couldn't quite explain she felt herself go slightly weak at the knees and decided that she ought to get back to helping with the tea.

Chapter Two

S'luvverly!

As Claire carried the tea-tray into the living-room she noticed the unpleasant smell again. It was stronger now. Which was strange, because Wendy was still in the garage. And it didn't smell like one of his pongs. This was a musty, earthy whiff, like the maggots her dad used for fishing bait.

Grandpa Reg had just reached the 'And these are my awards . . .' stage of the puddingathon. He had stacks: certificates of excellence, silver puddings, rosettes, testimonials from TV chefs . . . all kinds!

'Good graciousness!' exclaimed Hildegard. 'You heff done vell, Grandpa Vej! Your puddings must be very special. Could I be peeping at your recipes?'

'Not on your Nelly, yer can't! Yer cheeky

little monkey!' cried Grandpa, in his usual tactful manner. 'Them recipes is secret, lass. Harker's pudding recipes have been in t'family nigh on three hundred years. They're only ever passed on by word a mouth. I've got every one locked up in me noddle!'

'Including all his new ones,' said Mr Whimsy.

'Yup! They're all in here,' said Grandpa, tapping his head vigorously. 'Spicy Thai, Pork Tikka, Creole Coconut. The lot! We're very "go ahead" at Harker's!'

'Zat is so impressive,' said Dr Bruno. 'So Mr Sausage – err, I mean, Grandpa, vare is your famous pudding factory?'

'Right next t'river Eck,' said Grandpa Reg. 'In the old days they loaded t'puddings on to boats then sailed 'em out to sea. People all over t'world'd be waiting for 'em.'

'By Eck?' said Dr Bruno, suddenly looking more interested than ever.

'Yes lad! And by gum! And by jingo!' said Grandpa. 'I thought you'd be impressed. Harker's puddings are famous t'world over!'

'No! I mean, ze big sailing boats,' said Dr Bruno. 'Can zey come all ze way up to Chumley by ze River Eck?'

'By 'eck, of course they can,' cried Grandpa impatiently. 'Now, forget blinkin'

Eck and listen to this! When Captain Cook met the locals on the Pacific island of Fijitynesia, his very first words were . . .'

'OK playmates! Who's for a nice black pudding sarnie?'

It wasn't Captain Cook who said this. It was Claire's mum, breezing in with a huge plate of sandwiches.

'Oh, please yes!' said Dr Bruno excitedly. 'I am hungry enough to eat a hearse!'

'He means a horse!' smiled Hildegard, playfully elbowing Bruno in the ribs.

'Well, the Co-op was fresh out of them,' joked Mum, putting the plate in front of Bruno and Hildegard. 'So it'll just have to be black pudding sandwiches! Dig in folks. They're one of Grandpa's specials.'

Bruno was desperate. With a cry of, 'Toodle pips, up ze hatch!' he grabbed the biggest sarnie he could find, stuffed it into his enormous mouth, and began chomping away like he'd not eaten for weeks. However, a couple of moments later his face froze in an expression of pure terror and his eyes bulged as if they were popping out of their sockets.

'Oh donkerkrind, bluttersnap, my goot gutties. Hik, hik, hik!' he gasped, clutching wildly at his throat.

'Oh dear!' cried Claire's mum, as Bruno

slowly slid off the settee, spluttering and gagging.

'Heng on, my darlink! I am comink!' shrieked Hildegard, and she threw herself on top of Bruno, then began pummelling his huge chest with her sharp little fists. This made him splutter and gasp even more and soon bits of half-chewed sandwich were flying everywhere.

Ignoring the sarnie storm, Hildegard seized Bruno by the chin, thrust her hand deep into his throat and started fishing frantically as if she'd just dropped her best diamond necklace down there. A second later, she yelled triumphantly and pulled out what was left of the sandwich. She sniffed it, hurled it to the floor and began jumping up and down on it as if it were some deadly insect. After about two minutes, she stopped then joined Bruno on the settee again.

As the Whimsys stared in complete astonishment, Hildegard flashed a sweet little smile and said, 'He is sometimes such a silly! So many times heff I warned him not to be biting off more than he can be chewing! Zat bit of sendvich must have gone down ze wrong hole.' She suddenly stood up again and said, 'OK! So anyvay, we must be off. We have got a busy day behind us tomorrow!'

Five minutes later the Whimsys were waving farewell and watching the Blodvats' gigantic car slide out of their drive.

'What a lovely couple!' said Mr Whimsy.

'And so sophisticated!' said Mrs Whimsy

'Pity about the black puddin' sarnies though,' said Grandpa. 'That new triple garlic recipe didn't go down at all well, did it? What did you think of it, Claire?'

But Claire wasn't listening. She'd just been up to the bathroom and discovered that someone had taken the tops off all their deodorants, perfumes and aftershaves and helped themselves to at least half their contents. She'd also noticed that the very large bottle of Goldenbronze Factor 20 sun screen, which her mum and dad had taken on their French holiday, was now missing from the cabinet.

As she thought about their strange guests and their even stranger behaviour Claire got the distinct feeling she'd be seeing them again quite soon.

But she didn't know just *how* soon . . .

It was 2 a.m. and the Blodvats had been gone five hours, but Wendy's fur was still bristling and he was trembling from nose to tail as he lay curled up on the end of Claire's bed. Every now and again he would let out a low growl and turn his frightened eyes to the wall that separated Claire's room from Grandpa Reg's.

And *then* Claire heard it.

A low moaning suddenly came from Grandpa Reg's room, followed by excited muttering. Wendy dived under Claire's covers. Claire gave her petrified pet a reassuring pat then slipped out of bed and tiptoed across her room. As she stepped on to the landing she got a whiff of that awful, musty, maggoty smell again. But this time it was mixed with a familiar perfume – *Smooch*, her mum's favourite.

The door to Grandpa's room was partly open. Claire pressed herself against the landing wall and edged towards it. 'Probably nothing!' she told herself. 'But I'll take a look, just to be sure!' Very cautiously, she peeped into Grandpa's room. His toes were sticking out from under his blanket, twitching and jerking inside the red Chumley Rovers football socks he always wore in bed. But the rest of him was hidden by the sinister caped figure that was bending over him. The figure that was so absorbed in whatever awful thing it was doing that it didn't even notice when Claire gasped with terror.

She froze, unable to move or speak, clutching the door frame and gaping at the dreadful scene before her. A moment later, the figure sighed and raised its head from Grandpa's neck – just enough for Claire to recognize the chalk-white face, crimson lips and needle teeth of Mrs Blodvat. Uuurrrgh! Whatever was this horrible woman doing in her grandpa's room? Then Claire saw the red dribble on Hildegard's chin. And the truth hit her. Hildegard Blodvat had been sucking Grandpa Reg's blood.

As Claire struggled to recover from the shock of her dreadful discovery, Mrs Blodvat licked her lips greedily and looked towards the window. Hovering in mid-air, like an enormous, bloated black bat, was Dr Bruno. He grinned stupidly at Hildegard, pointed to Grandpa, licked his own lips, then waggled his eyebrows. Mrs Blodvat put her thumb up and winked, as if to say, 'Yes, a very good vintage!' Then she bent over Grandpa and sank her teeth into his neck again.

I've got to do something! thought Claire. I can't let this monstrous creature suck my grandpa dry. He's probably not got much blood to spare, what with being seventy-five and having shed most of it for King and country!

The Blodvats hadn't seen her yet. Claire decided to charge into the room and knock Hildegard for six before she could do more harm to dear old Grandpa. But at that moment Grandpa Reg suddenly put his arms around Mrs Blodvat's neck and said, 'Ooh by gum – that's smashing, love! Do it some more! S'luvverly!'

Claire could hardly believe it. Grandpa was talking to Mrs Blodvat! And cuddling her. And apparently enjoying the horrid thing she was doing to him.

'I'd never realized you was such a good kisser,' murmured Grandpa, as Hildegard struggled to free herself from his embrace. 'But ever since I chatted you up at the bus stop outside the Co-op, I've always fancied you. And I'm dead chuffed you've packed Tommy Pickles in. Even though he is my best mate!'

Then Claire realized Grandpa Reg was dreaming. He'd gone back to the days when he was first going out with Granny Dot. Hildegard Blodvat's nasty nocturnal neck-nibbling activities must have given him the impression he was in the middle of a passionate 1950s snogging session! All of a sudden, Grandpa Reg sat straight up in bed, seized Hildegard by her shoulders and yelled, 'WILL YER MARRY ME, DOROTHY? I know I'm only on two shillings and sixpence a week at the black pudding factory, but Mr Rathbone says I've a great future in offal. Please say you will, me duck!' And then he gave her a smacking great kiss on her forehead.

Mrs Blodvat looked absolutely panic-stricken. Without warning, she began to vibrate all over. In just seconds she turned from a solid, all-biting, all-sucking mini-woman, to a mysterious wisp of blue mist. A wisp that slid from Grandpa's grasp, floated across the room, passed through the tiny window ventilator and out into the night air, where it joined Bruno, who was bobbing around like a demented helicopter. As quickly as she'd mistified herself, Mrs Blodvat de-mistified. Then, with a couple of flicks of their massive, bat-wing capes, the two awful Blodvats were flapping their way across the rooftops of Chumley-by-Eck.

Mum and Dad will never believe this! thought Claire as she watched the silhouettes pass across the face of the moon and finally disappear from sight.

She rushed in to Grandpa Reg. He now looked completely bewildered as his hands clutched desperately at the space where Hildegard had been. Thankfully, he still seemed to be fast asleep. And apart from some scratches on his neck (even smaller than the razor nicks he regularly gave himself whilst shaving), he seemed none the worse for wear. Claire certainly didn't want to wake him. There was no telling what harm that would do. She gently patted his hand and said, "'S all right, Grandpa. She's gone now.'

Grandpa Reg shrugged, mumbled something about plenty more fish in the sea, snuggled down, and began snoring again.

'Yes! Such a lovely couple!' Claire murmured, remembering her parents' words of a few hours earlier, as she looked out at the night sky.

Chapter Three

The British Vampire

The following day at school, Claire's teacher, Mr Pither, asked her the name of the huge group of countries which Britain had once dominated. And she immediately said, 'The British Vampire!' It just came out that way. She was so busy worrying about the answers to her *own* questions, like: was what she'd seen the night before real, or a dream? And if it hadn't been a dream and there really were a couple of vampires in Chumley, who should she tell? The police? Her parents? The pest control man at the local council? She supposed it ought to be her mum and dad – which wouldn't be easy. The last thing they'd want to hear was that their lovely new friends were a pair of vampires.

She made a decision. Before she said

anything to anyone she'd have to find out more. So that evening she paid a visit to Chumley Library.

'Err, excuse me, have you got any books about vampires?' she asked the librarian.

'My goodness!' he replied. 'You're the fourth person this week. All our vampire books are out. But why don't you search on our Internet terminal. There's bound to be information there!'

Claire was about to say she'd got her own computer but decided that she might as well use the library one. When she tapped 'Vampires' into the search engine it came up with a huge list. Quite a lot were ads for stuff like joke vampire clothing and a fair few were complete rubbish, but after persevering she found a really useful looking site called http://www.all-things-strange-and-terrible She followed the links and finally clicked on a section called . . .

She thought of printing it off but when she saw it ran to more than forty pages she decided to make her own notes instead . . .

Vampires are found the world over. They are neither dead nor alive. To survive, they must drink the blood of living people. Sometimes they drink the blood of animals such as cows, horses and dogs. Vampires are also known as the 'undead' or 'Nosferatu', which means 'plague carrier'.

Uuurgh – disgusting! Claire thought, and shuddered violently when she realized that a couple of undead people may well have been drinking tea in her front room. She quickly wrote herself a reminder to give all the cups a good scrub with really strong disinfectant the moment she got home.

Next she read . . .

People believe they will recognize a vampire by their fangs. Wrong! Most vampires have retractable fangs. It is also a mistake to think they always wear black capes with high standing collars. Most of the time they wear normal clothes. In addition to which, they can be quite charming.

She recalled Dr Bruno's icy lips on her fingers and gave an even bigger shudder. Then, with an enormous sigh of relief, she read . . .

Today, most educated people believe there's no such thing as a vampire. Folklore experts say they were a myth dreamed up by ignorant, over-imaginative people in days gone by. However, some experts believe vampires do exist. They say there are just so many thousands of records of vampire incidents that there just has to be some truth in them.

Uh oh! she thought and quickly clicked on 'Protecting Yourself From Vampires', which began . .

Vampires are very frightened of the special holy biscuits known as eucharistic wafers.

Bet they don't sell them in Chumley Co-op! Claire thought. It continued . . .

If there's one thing vampires really hate, it's garlic!

Ah, she thought, no wonder Bruno didn't like his sarnie!

Next she clicked on 'Vampires as Shape Shifters' and read . . .

Vampires have incredible powers of transformation. They are able to turn themselves into cats, bats, dogs, frogs, wisps of mist, snakes and other 'natural' things at the drop of a hat.
See below:

Yup! thought Claire. That's Mrs Blodvat! She read on . . .

In order to become airborne all ordinary vampires must transform themselves into flying creatures like bats, owls or insects. However, one sort of undead that can fly in its natural vampire state is the 'ubervampire' – the vampire elite who is said to rule the entire undead world. This small, powerful and mysterious group is thought to be made up of two or three of the oldest of all vampire families, However, apart from that, little is known about it.

As Claire read this her flesh crept. Being menaced by ordinary undead had felt bad enough! But now it looked like her family were under threat from some sort of super-vampires! She rapidly scrolled to . . .

How to spot a vampire:

1) Vampires are cold to the touch – however, do not handle a vampire.

2) The eyes of vampires take on a terrifying red glow when they get angry or excited.

3) Certain vampires have no shadows. This sort can turn ordinary people into vampires simply by stealing their shadows.

4) The best way to recognize a vampire is by its awful smell – a musty, maggoty stink that comes from being neither dead nor alive and spending lots of time in dark, damp, smelly places like coffins and crypts.

Now Claire was one hundred per cent certain. The Blodvats just had to be vampires! There was no forgetting that awful pong. In fact, her nostrils were filling up with it right now.

'Hello, my dear,' said a voice like lemon juice. 'Doing a little homework?'

Claire looked up. Hildegard Blodvat was standing next to her. And looking at the on-screen display with the greatest of interest.

'Mrs Blodvat!' gasped Claire. 'What are you doing here?'

'Reading,' said Hildegard. 'Like you. You look pale. Are you all right?'

'Yes, nothing wrong with m-me,' stammered Claire. 'I'm all white! P-perfectly all white – I mean all right!'

She wasn't, of course. She was panic-stricken. In a desperate attempt to hide the vampire page she spread her fingers across the screen and grinned up at Hildegard pathetically. Then she tried hitting the off-button, but that brought up an on-screen message: 'Are you sure you want to close down? A network operation is in progress.'

'YES!' yelled Claire. ''Course I do! Why do you think I pressed your "off" button?'

'Let me,' crooned Hildegard. She calmly clicked the mouse and the site disappeared.

'Err, thanks,' said Claire, giving Hildegard another pathetic grin.

Hildegard grinned back then quickly reached for Claire's note book, saying, 'Ah! This is a subject I know a liddle about. Maybe I can enlighten you?'

Claire slammed her note pad shut, trapping Hildegard's fingers. 'No! No thanks!' she blurted out. 'It's all right. I've found what

I wanted. For my homework all about imaginary beings. Anyway, I've got to go. I'll be late for my breakfast! Lunch! Haircut! Tea?'

'Black puddings!' said the librarian.

'No, not now, thanks,' said Claire.

'Actually, I was talking to this lady,' said the librarian, handing Hildegard a pile of books. 'I think these might help you,' he continued. 'I couldn't find Eck navigation charts but we do have lots of books on black pudding making.' Then he added proudly, 'After all, Chumley is the world centre of the blood sausage industry!'

Claire seized her opportunity. 'I'll be off then, Mrs Blodvat. Ta ta!' She quickly stood up and began backing towards the exit.

Hildegard glanced up from the book the librarian was showing her, flashed Claire the sort of look that can melt a granite paving stone and then, in a very meaningful voice, she said, 'Do take care, dear.'

'Of course,' said the librarian, fussing over the books importantly. 'I am a qualified archivist. Now, as you're not a member you won't be able to take these away with you. But you're welcome to read them in the library. Please be very careful with them.'

As Claire slipped through the library

doors she thought she heard Hildegard give a long, low hiss, closely followed by a high pitched squeak of terror from the librarian. But she couldn't be sure.

Outside it was dark and raining heavily. Claire dashed down High Street, not daring to look behind her. By the time she reached Eck Street the rain was easing but a thin low mist was drifting in off the river. When she finally turned into Blood Pudding Lane the rain had stopped and the mist was much thicker, but still only at waist height. Almost there, she thought, as she raced towards the black pudding works. Five minutes and I'll be home.

Then something made her stop dead. Just twenty metres ahead the silhouette of Harker's Black Pudding Factory loomed up out of the mist. Making its way up the front wall was a large, dark shape, moving very cautiously and slowly, like an enormous black beetle. Occasionally, it would pause, move its huge head from side to side, then continue its slow, slow ascent of the wall.

Claire ducked into the alley opposite the factory and watched its progress with horrified fascination. How could anything, or anyone, for that matter, climb that wall? It was at least thirty metres high. There was nothing to cling on to but the sheer brick face, and that would be really slippery from the rain. The thing stopped at the fourth storey window, peered in, then turned its head and looked down.

Claire found herself staring up at the big lardy face of Dr Blodvat. For one awful moment she thought he'd seen her. But he hadn't. As she continued to watch in awestruck horror, his outline began to shimmer and blur, before melting into a wisp of blue vapour that slipped through a ventilator grille and disappeared.

As Claire crouched in the alley, wondering what to do next, her attention was distracted by a movement at the end of Blood

Pudding Lane. A large car was sliding silently and sinisterly towards the sausage factory. As the monstrous Mercedes drew close Claire could see Hildegard's weaselly, wicked face peering through the spokes of the steering wheel while her claw-like hands gripped its rim a couple of inches above her eyebrows.

The Mercedes drew to a halt and Hildegard gave three gentle toots on the horn. Moments later a light came on and Dr Bruno appeared at the fourth-floor window holding a large black sausage which he waved triumphantly. Hildegard smiled up at him, then tooted the horn again, only this time with more urgency.

She's come to warn Bruno they've been rumbled, thought Claire. He's had to cut short his sausage snatching operation. He vaporized again and a jumbo-sized black pudding floated eerily through the ventilator, followed closely by a blue wisp. A second later Bruno reformed as his sinister, solid shape, placed the stolen sausage between his teeth, then began to descend the wall the way he'd come – head first!

Claire was astounded. How could such an enormous man do such a thing? On reaching the ground he slithered across the wet pavement. The car's rear passenger door swung open and he slipped inside. With a squeal of tyres, the Mercedes shot off down Blood Pudding Lane.

Oh no! she thought. I'm done for. Hildegard knows that I know. And now they're after me!

Chapter Four
The Blodcats

Claire took a deep breath, summoned all her courage and set off for home. She hurried along the near-deserted streets, her mind racing wildly through the events of the last twenty-four hours. The Blodvats were *definitely* vampires! And they hadn't come to Chumley just to say 'Hi!' to her parents.

It was Grandpa and the sausage factory they were interested in. Which made sense. Black puddings were made of pigs' blood, and vampires were addicted to blood. But the website had said they drank animal blood only very occasionally. It was human blood they were crazy about.

Suddenly, a horrible thought struck Claire. Surely the Blodvats weren't planning to make sausages out of—? No! That was just too terrible even to think about. She tried to concentrate on other clues. Like that graveyard guide and those curious doodles in the atlas. And the questions about the Eck. Maybe the sausage snatching operation was part of something much,. much bigger! But what? Only one thing was certain. The Blodvats meant danger. *Terrible* danger.

Claire finally turned the corner into her street, then paused for a second before walking the last hundred metres to her house. The Blodvats could pop up from behind a hedge at any moment, or sneak up and drag her off before she uttered a sound. She scanned the street. There was no sign of the Blodmobile. But they'd probably hidden the car in some lonely spot so they could bundle her into it without being seen.

Claire began to walk towards her house. Just as she was beginning to think she might get home safely, a very odd-looking pair of black cats suddenly materialized out of the low swirling mist. One was huge and powerful, the other, tiny and skinny. They were two houses from hers and looking up and down the street as if expecting someone.

Claire knew all the cats round her way and she'd never ever seen this pair of odd bods before! Suddenly she remembered the vampire web pages and got a terrible sinking feeling in the pit of her stomach . . .

> Vampires have incredible powers of transformation. They are able to turn themselves into cats, bats, dogs, frogs, wisps of mist, snakes and various other 'natural' things at the drop of a hat.

The Blodvats had turned themselves into cats. Or, more precisely – Blodcats! The smaller cat's glittery green eyes were the spitting image of Hildegard Blodvat's. Claire thought of hopping over a neighbour's fence and sneaking up to her house through the gardens. But too late! The Blodcats had spotted her and were now purposefully padding her way, backs arched, tails in the air. Of course, anyone else seeing them would assume they were ordinary moggies. But Claire knew better.

The menacing moggies were just a couple of metres from her now. If only I had some garlic, she thought. Or one of those holy biscuit thingies. Then she remembered she still had a chocolate digestive left over from her lunch. Maybe the Blodvats wouldn't spot the difference if she kept the chocolate side hidden. Claire swung her bag from her shoulder, reached into her lunchbox and took out the digestive.

The cats were almost within striking distance. Claire stood perfectly still with her feet slightly apart then gripped the biscuit in her left hand and thrust it in front of her like a shield. The cats halted, looked slightly confused, then continued to pad towards her.

'Dr Bruno!' screamed Claire. 'Get back! And don't you come any closer either, Hildegard! This biscuit's, err—' She almost said 'loaded!' then thought better of it and said, 'got special powers!'

Completely ignoring Claire's warning, the tiny cat suddenly twitched its tail and did a couple of quick, playful skips that brought it within centimetres of her feet. As it did, she jumped back and yelled, 'Don't try anything funny! I saw what you did to Grandpa! Leave me alone!' Her shouts caused the smaller cat to stop, but the large one kept coming. Then without warning it did two leaps and bounced past her. Then Claire stepped back and shook the chocolate digestive at it threateningly.

The little cat went into a low menacing crouch, waggled its bottom twice, then pounced on Claire's left trainer, seizing the laces between its teeth.

'Get your fangs off me!' Claire screamed. 'You can't hurt me. Don't you realize what kind of biscuit this is?'

At that moment a powerful hand grasped her shoulder and a low, menacing voice whispered, 'Yes! A chocolate digestive! Ha ha! Got you now!'

'Dad!' gasped Claire. 'What are you doing here?'

'Err – this is where I live!' laughed Mr Whimsy, letting go of her shoulder. 'What are you up to?'

'I've been to the library,' mumbled Claire. 'To do some . . . research.'

'What on?' said her dad. 'How to talk Moggy? Why ever were you shouting mumbo jumbo at these cats? I'm sure I heard you call one Mrs Blodcat.'

'Mrs Bad Cat! As a joke. Ha ha!'

'Hmm, hilarious,' said her dad, giving her an odd look. 'Enough to make a cat laugh. But more to the point, why were you waving that biscuit at them? I don't think they go for digestives. Do you, puss?'

Mr Whimsy reached down to stroke the small cat, which was now rubbing against his ankle.

'DAD! DON'T DO THAT!' yelled Claire, grabbing his arm. 'Don't touch it! It's not an ordinary cat. It's really Mrs—'

'Taylor's,' said her dad, tickling the cat's neck while it snuggled his foot and purred encouragingly. 'The woman who's just moved into number thirty.'

'I didn't know she has cats,' said Claire. 'I've not seen any.'

43

'She's been keeping them indoors,' said her dad, picking up the big cat and tickling its ears. 'She didn't want them trying to find their way back to their old house. They've got their new address tags on now. Haven't you, you softy?'

As the cat snuggled up to him, Mr Whimsy turned over its name-tag. It said, *Sooty Taylor, 30 Whitby Gardens, Chumley.*

'Oh yes, I see what you mean,' said Claire, feeling foolish. 'But in that case, where are the Blodvats?'

'When I came out to post my letter they were at our place, talking to Mum and Grandpa Reg,' said her dad. 'But I suspect they might be making tracks.' He looked down the road and said, 'Talk of the devil, here they are now!'

The Blodvats' car had just pulled out of the Whimsys' drive. Bruno tooted the horn and Hildegard waved cheerily. But Claire wasn't looking at them. She was staring at a small, familiar figure in the back. It was Grandpa Reg, wearing his best red blazer and official 'Grand Pudding-Masters' tie and looking extremely pleased with himself. As the car sped past he gave her the thumbs up. A moment later the Blodmobile was gone.

'Dad,' said Claire, as they walked up their

44

drive. 'What's Grandpa Reg doing in the Blodmobile – I mean, Mercedes?'

'They're taking him for a flying visit,' said her dad.

'A what?' exclaimed Claire, remembering the Blodvats' moonlit flit.

'A car ride to Moaning Man Moor and the Eck Estuary. He's showing them the sites and giving them the local legends lowdown.'

'In the dark?'

'Why not? Grandpa's always said those spooky old places are best seen by moonlight. They'll probably visit the catacombs up on Crawley Common. And Ravenscrag graveyard. Bruno and Hildegard really dig old burial grounds.'

'Yes,' said Claire. 'I'm sure they do! Err . . . when will they be back?'

'No telling! Afterwards Bruno and Hildegard are taking Grandpa back to their digs for drinks.'

Yes, thought Claire with a shudder, I bet they are!

Chapter Five
Piece of Cake!

After dinner Claire went to her room to do her homework. But, try as she might, she couldn't concentrate. She kept thinking about Grandpa Reg. In the end she gave up and logged on to http://www.all-things-strange-and-terrible then began reading 'Vampires and their Victims' . . .

Vampires always need victims. The more blood they suck, the stronger they become. Reasons for choosing victims:

A) Pleasure   B) Power   C) Revenge

Vampires rarely kill victims but often attack them repeatedly. This leads to the victim becoming drained of energy, and pale and miserable. Three bites in three places in one single attack will usually turn a victim into a vampire.

Claire wondered how many times Hildegard's horrible fangs had already pierced Grandpa Reg's wrinkled old skin. It just didn't bear thinking about. She rapidly scrolled to 'Vampires and Mind Control' . . .

Most vampires have telepathic and hypnotic powers which they use to bring victims and those around them under their control. For example, they use hypnosis to make victims forget attacks. They will also employ their powers to tranquillize and gain the trust of a victim's friends and family.

Her parents' words echoed through her mind, 'Such a lovely couple!' Had *they* been tranquillized?

Next she moved to 'Vampires at Rest' . . .

Vampires sleep for anything between a day and a decade. However, some have been known to sleep for whole centuries. Vampires who spend a really long time underground often gnaw their own fingers and toes.

Claire suddenly had an image of Bruno's right hand with its missing fingertips and felt quite ill. She quickly moved on . . .

Many people think that vampires sleep in the daytime and come out at night. This is not always the case. Although they are sensitive to strong light, many vampires do hunt in the day. However, as sunlight increases their strength decreases. To get proper rest vampires travelling abroad must sleep in earth from their homelands.

As Claire took in this terrifying information, the day's events flashed through her mind, like a video nightmare on constant play. She kept seeing Hildegard in the library; Bruno climbing the factory wall; those pesky pussies padding towards her.

Most of all, she saw Grandpa Reg in the Blodmobile, looking so happy because he was off on an outing with his pals. And now she just couldn't stop worrying about him. They'd been gone for ages. In that time the Blodvats could have done anything. Dangled him from a tree then drained his blood into a bucket – slowly! Or taken him to some sort of vampire blood and cheese evening and passed him around their friends so they could all have a taste then comment on his flavour. And if anything bad had happened it would be her fault.

Oh, why hadn't she said something to her parents when she'd seen him in the Blodmobile? All it needed was a word and they could have raced after the Blodvats and intercepted them. Maybe caught them mid-guzzle! But now it was probably too late.

Or was it? Claire suddenly remembered what Grandpa Reg had once said when she'd been worried over some schoolwork she was late handing in. 'Claire,' he'd said. 'It's never too late. Where there's a will, there's a way!'

He was right! There was still time to save him. All she had to do was convince her parents the Blodvats were vampires. Ha! Piece of cake!

When she went into the sitting room, her mum and dad were watching the newsreader blathering on about a series of tube train stoppages in London. Hmm, she thought. They think they've got problems!

She knew this wouldn't be easy. Telling your parents you suspected their new friends of being recently risen vampires, who were probably planning to drink them drier than a couple of packets of powdered milk, and were no doubt doing the same thing to your grandfather at that very moment just wasn't the sort of thing you did every day.

'Err – Mum, Dad?' she said, as casually as she could, 'Can I have a word with you about Bruno and Hildegard?'

"Course you can,' said Mum.

'So,' said Mr Whimsy. 'What is it?'

'Well,' said Claire. 'I think they may not be exactly what they appear to be. If you know what I mean.'

As she said 'know' she waggled her eyebrows and jiggled her head in the desperate hope that her parents might realize what she was getting at and say something like, 'Oh, you're talking about them being vampires. We know that, dear! Live and let live, is what we say! And don't worry about Grandpa. They've promised not to harm him.' But her mum just said, 'Claire, stop twitching! Have you got fleas?'

Then Dad said, 'So, what are they then?'

'Dead!' said Claire, as calmly as she could.

'Dead?' said Mr Whimsy. 'Dead what? Dead nice? Dead rich? Dead boring? What sort of dead?'

'No, just dead!' said Claire. 'Actually, I don't mean dead. Because they aren't properly dead! They're more sort of un–un–un—' She was desperate to say undead, but it wouldn't come out. She tried again. 'Look, what I'm trying to say is that Bruno and Hildegard are a pair of un–un—'

'Underpants?' said her dad.

Claire shook her head furiously. 'No, they're un–un—'

'Onions?' said her mum.

Claire shook her head even harder.

'Unlucky?' said her dad. 'Under the weather? Are we getting warm?'

'Come on, Claire,' laughed her mum. 'Give us a clue!'

Claire couldn't believe it. What was meant to have been a serious and urgent talk had suddenly turned into some sort of stupid TV game show.

'Stop! Stop!' she cried. 'This is ridiculous. I feel like I'm going to blow up!'

'Aha!' cried Mr Whimsy. 'Got it! It's unexploded bombs, isn't it? Brilliant! You think Hildegard and Bruno are a pair of unexploded bombs. Ha ha! I win!'

It was useless. She'd have to stop dithering. She took a deep breath and said, 'Listen, Mum and Dad, in my opinion your new friends are neither dead nor alive. What's more, I think they must be at least three hundred years old. To be honest with you, I think Bruno and Hildegard are nothing more than a pair of . . . *walking corpses!*'

There was a long stunned silence. Mrs Whimsy was the first to speak. 'Claire,' she gasped. 'What would Bruno and Hildegard think if they could hear you now? I've a good mind to send you to your room!'

'Hang on a minute,' said her dad, always the calmer of her parents. 'I realize you think a lot of our friends are boring and ancient. But to describe Bruno and Hildegard as "walking corpses" is bit much! They may not be your idea of fun but we find them jolly good company!'

'No, no!' cried Claire. 'You still don't understand. What I'm trying to say is that I think the Blodvats are ... VAMPIRES! Have you seen Bruno's hand? His fingertips are all missing. You know where they went, don't you?'

'Where?' said Mum.

'He ate them!' said Claire. 'Gnawed them off!' She nibbled her own fingers ferociously, just to make sure they understood.

'Ate them?' said Mum. 'Why?'

'Because he was starving!' said Claire. 'After he'd been in his box too long. He's probably chewed off three or four of his toes too!'

'Actually, Claire,' her dad said quite calmly, 'I happen to know Bruno didn't eat his fingers. He lost them at Castle Blodvat, in an accident with a grape-crushing machine.' Then, with a concerned look, he leaned forward and took Claire's hands in his. 'Listen, Claire,' he said. 'I think we need a chat.'

'Why, Dad?' said Claire. But she knew what was coming.

'Well,' said her dad. 'Ever since you were little you've had a very active imagination. And an interest in things that are, er, out of the ordinary.'

'Weird is what I'd say,' said her mum. 'And you're highly strung.'

'Mum!' said Claire. 'I'm a girl, not a line of washing!'

'The thing is, Claire,' continued her dad, 'imagination isn't always a good thing. For instance, do you remember the night you saw the werewolf prowling around our garden? Or the alsatian from the chip shop, as most people round here call it.'

'How was I to know?' said Claire. 'It'd been staring up at my bedroom window for ages!'

'It wasn't you it was after! It was Wendy, his pal.'

'But Dad!' cried Claire. 'This time it's different! I just know I'm right! In fact I know that at this very moment Grandpa Reg is in terrible danger and that he's—'

'Absolutely gasping for a cuppa!' said a voice behind her.

'And that he's absolutely gasping for a

cuppa,' said Claire. She whirled around to see Grandpa Reg in the doorway, grinning from ear to ear.

'Whatever is this barmy girl going on about?' he laughed.

'Ooh, take no notice!' said Mum. 'She's off in cloud cuckoo land again. Now you sit down and I'll make you a nice brew. Have you had a good time with Bruno and Hildy?'

'Absolutely champion!' said Grandpa Reg, patting Wendy and flopping into his favourite armchair. 'We've seen the sights and had some laughs. Never a dull moment with old Bruno. Mind you, I had t'remind him about driving on the left a couple of times. Gave us some right frights! By the way, him and Hildegard asked me to apologize for them not coming in. They're making an early start tomorrow. They're off to Whitby for a few days. I've done them a nice route round all the interesting churchyards. I think they'll have a right good trip!'

'Oh, you are good,' said Mum as she came in with his tea.

'It's nice to think I'm of use,' said Grandpa Reg. He stretched, then yawned and said, 'Now, if it's all the same to you I think I'll take my cuppa up to bed, I'm cream crackered! Come to think of it, I've got a bit of a headache coming on!'

'Probably all the excitement,' said Dad.

'Yes,' Grandpa agreed. 'Probably all the excitement.'

A couple of days after the Blodvats left for Whitby, Grandpa Reg complained of being 'a bit under the weather'. The Whimsys knew he must be feeling bad because he couldn't even face his black pudding fritters. And he'd had them for brekky ever since the day he'd started work as an apprentice tripe stacker at Olliford's offal factory. So Mrs Whimsy sent him back to bed and rang for the doctor.

'Mr Harker's been overdoing it,' Claire heard Doctor Grainger telling Mum as he came downstairs after examining Grandpa Reg. 'He needs lots of rest.'

'Doesn't surprise me,' said Mrs Whimsy. 'He's been working his socks off on his new offal recipes.'

'Yes,' said Dr Grainger. 'He does appear to have been working *offally* hard! Ha ha ha!' And he laughed so much at his joke that he fell down the last five steps.

'Are you all right, Dr Grainger?' said Mrs Whimsy.

'I think so,' said Dr Grainger, getting to his feet.

'Maybe you ought to see a doctor,' said Mrs Whimsy.

Dr Grainger turned to the Whimsy's hall mirror and said, 'Ah, what luck! There's one now! I'm better already. Ha ha!'

'Oh you are a tonic, Dr Grainger,' laughed Claire's mum. 'I don't know how you stay so cheerful.'

'Well, Mrs Whimsy, you know what they say. Laughter's the best medicine! It works wonders for some of my patients. I just wish it would work on Mr Harker. I told him my best knock-knock joke and he didn't even smile.'

'Yes,' sighed Mrs Whimsy. 'And to think, a few days ago he had such a twinkle in his eye. By the way, did he tell you about his eyes?'

'Yes, but don't worry,' said Dr Grainger. 'Extra sensitivity to strong light is common at his age. Just make sure he keeps his bedroom curtains drawn and those dark glasses on. And tell him to look on the bright side!'

Before Mrs Whimsy could ask Dr Grainger if this was another joke, he added, 'And don't let his craving for tomato soup bother you. It'll help keep up his strength. By the way, he says can you bring him another bowl.'

'But that's his seventh this morning!'

So Grandpa Reg stayed in bed wearing his shades, drinking gallons of tomato soup and reading Westerns. The only time Claire saw him out of his room was when he shuffled around the house looking for a fresh book. Sometimes he'd vary his tomato soup diet with tomato juice, or tomato sauce!

Claire felt really sorry for him. Every now and again she'd pop into his room and challenge him to an arm wrestling match or a game of Connect Four but he usually muttered something about 'not being up to it' then he'd go back to reading *Two Guns for Texas*.

But she couldn't help feeling suspicious when, about three days after Dr Grainger's visit, Grandpa said, 'Claire, can I ask you something?'

''Course you can,' she said. 'Go ahead!'

Grandpa Reg pulled up the bedclothes until they almost covered his face then, in a small and pathetic-sounding voice, he said, 'I was wondering if you've ever had the urge to err . . . eat a fly?'

'No! Never!' said Claire, feeling rather shocked. 'Why – have you?'

''Course not!' he replied indignantly. What d'yer take me for? Some kinda fruitcake?'

'Then why did you ask me?' said Claire.

'I'm just making conversation,' said Grandpa Reg, then he turned over and opened *Broken Arrow*.

Claire didn't think any more about the fly question until the next evening when she went into his room and found him standing on a chair, jabbing at a spider's web with his walking stick, trying to hook out the dead bluebottles! He didn't even notice her come in.

'Grandpa!' she exclaimed. 'What are you doing?'

He whirled around so quickly that he nearly fell off the chair, then gave her a really guilty look and said, 'Er . . . spring cleaning!'

'But it's September!' said Claire.

'I know,' he said. 'I thought I'd make an early start.'

The next day Claire was helping her mum tidy Grandpa Reg's room while he was having his bath when she discovered his secret hoard. She was putting away his socks when she found a chocolate box hidden under his emergency woolly undies. As she lifted it to straighten his sock pile, she accidentally knocked off the lid and saw that it was full of creepy-crawlies.

There were more flies than anything but she could also see earwigs, daddy long legs, and woodlice. He'd sorted them into their various types by popping them into the compartments the chocolates had been in.

As soon as she'd re-hidden the box she nipped to her room and called up the vampire pages on her PC. Despite a thorough search, she couldn't find anything about vampires and fly eating, apart from one puzzling note which said, 'Flies – see Stoker'. Claire hadn't the foggiest idea who Stoker was so in the end she convinced herself that Grandpa Reg had collected the insects for fishing bait and pushed the whole matter to the back of her mind.

Then, two days later, Grandpa Reg began to improve. The Whimsys were delighted, especially when he said he fancied strolling down to the Pudding Maker's Arms and visiting Clackett's Fish Lounge for a cod supper as he was getting heartily sick of tomato soup. He even made a joke, saying that after his hibernation and red sauce diet it was time he went down the pub to 'ketchup on the news!' and Mrs Whimsy said, 'Yes, Dr Grainger's right – laughter is the best medicine!'

So the family breathed a sigh of relief because Grandpa Reg definitely seemed to be over the worst of his troubles. But then, around the time he had his second evening out on the town, something happened that made the Whimsys and quite a few other Chumleyites decide their streets were no longer safe for old folk to be out on their own. Nor, for that matter, anyone else.

Chapter Six

The Chumley Terror

laire found out about the horrific incident when she got home from school the following afternoon. Her mum was full of it and bursting to tell someone. As Chumley was a very quiet sort of place where someone's lost glove could make front page headlines in the *Echo*, then be the talk of the town for weeks, Claire and Dad were all ears.

'Have you heard what happened after the Senior Citizens' Horlicks and Hobbies Evening?' said Mum, hardly able to contain herself. 'Mrs Tibshelf and Miss Eggerton had just finished their Karate class and were on their way to Clackett's for their usual cod and curry sauce when they noticed a mysterious figure leaping out of alleyways and stamping on their shadows, like it wanted to trap them.

'When they turned to see what the kerfuffle was, it would dodge into an alley, only to turn up a bit further on and do it again. After a while it gave up and disappeared so they thought no more of it. However, just as they turned into Whitby Road they heard a cry so terrifying it made their blood turn to slush! Miss Eggerton said it was a yell, but Mrs Tibshelf thought it was a howl.'

'Probably a yowl!' said Dad. 'Possibly like this?' Then he let out such a terrifying 'YOWL' that Wendy leapt straight from his basket into the kitchen sink.

'Yes!' said Mum, lifting Wendy out of the washing-up water and wringing him out. 'A yowl! And there, hovering above them, was this terrifying creature! A horrible half-human, half-thing thing.'

'So was it flying?' said Claire, alarmed.

''Course not!' said Mum. 'It stood on the bakery wall. At first Mrs Tibshelf paid it no attention because she thought it was barmy Ted Warburton from the Over Seventies' Karaoke Society doing his Elvis impression but then she remembered Ted was staying in Derby with his son Trevor so she thought she ought to start screaming.'

'What!' said Dad. 'Just because Ted Warburton had gone to stay with Trevor?'

'No, you chump!' said Mum. 'Because she and Miss Eggerton were being menaced by a fiend the likes of which has never been seen before in Chumley!'

'By 'eck!' said Dad.

'All right: Never seen before in Chumley-by-Eck!'

'No,' said Dad. 'I mean, by 'eck! this is exciting! So what did this fiend look like?'

'Miss Eggerton said it had a furry head and bulging black eyes and huge leathery wings like a pterodactyl's. But Mrs Tibshelf disagreed,' said Mum. 'She said it had a balaclava and wrap-around sunglasses on, like they wear in *Baywatch*.'

'They don't wear balaclavas in *Baywatch*,' said Dad.

'And it was wearing a big, black, cyclist's rain cape,' said Mum.

'Hmmph!' said Dad. 'So, whose description was right? Mrs Tibshelf's or Miss Eggerton's?'

'Well, what with their specs being steamed up, they weren't sure. But they did agree about its teeth! They were like daggers. Miss Eggerton said they made her knees knock like a flamenco dancer's maracas. She's been showing them to all and sundry all day long.'

'What! – her knees?' said Dad.

'No, the teeth! Haven't you seen that queue outside the Post Office? That's what they're all waiting to see.'

'But wouldn't that be a bit difficult,' said Dad, 'with them being attached to the fiend?'

'They aren't,' said Mum. 'Not any more. As those two old dears gibbered pitifully, the fiend suddenly opened its mouth and did another of those horrendous—'

'YOWLS!' yowled Dad, causing Wendy to jump into the sink for the second time that evening.

'And that's when its teeth fell out on to the pavement,' said Mum. 'Mrs Tibshelf scooped them up in a flash, then waved them at him and said, "I've got your choppers, Fungus Bonce. Come and get them if you're hard enough." That's when he fell off the wall.'

'Fell off the wall?'

'Yes! He tumbled into the big bin where the bakery bungs its mouldy muffins. Mrs Tibshelf was going to slam the lid down and take him prisoner but by the time she'd climbed over the wall he'd scrambled out and scarpered. And that was that!'

'Wow!' said Dad. 'What a story! Chumley's not seen this much excitement since Derek Tindersley's underpants caught fire halfway through his spin and rinse cycle.' Then he looked glum and said, 'And I suppose that'll be it for at least the next ten years!'

Don't be so sure, thought Claire. I reckon Chumley's troubles are only just beginning . . .

At school the next day everyone was talking about the Chumley Terror. Half of them wanted to believe the Terror had been real while the other half said it was probably someone playing a trick, especially as those teeth turned out to be plastic. Claire decided to keep quiet about the whole matter so she just stood and listened to various brave bods describe what they'd do if they met the Terror and how it was time things livened up in Chumley, anyway.

By the time afternoon break arrived the topics of teeth and terror were more or less exhausted so everyone went back to their usual pastime of 'kick it and run', or football, as the pretentious ones liked to call it. As they were kicking off Claire realized she'd left her gloves in the classroom so she popped back for them.

As she did she noticed Jason Turner sitting at his table looking really fed up.

Jason never missed a football game and as far as Claire knew, probably played it in his sleep. Something was wrong.

'Hi, Jason!' she said. 'Why aren't you playing footy?'

'Groin injury,' said Jason, pointing to his chest.

'That's your breastbone,' said Claire. 'Your groin's further down.'

'It spread!' said Jason.

'Come off it, Jason!' said Claire. 'There's something else, isn't there?'

'Well, yes there is,' said Jason. 'I'm worried about my dad. He's been acting really peculiar just lately. He looks different, too. His skin's gone sort of pale. And he's started wearing loads of black. Black shirts, braces, scarves, trousers, undies, hats – the lot.'

'But what about the day-glo track suits, the year-round tan and the trainers that would put a prawn cocktail to shame?' said Claire. 'Doesn't he go in for that sort of thing any more?'

'You must be kidding,' said Jason. 'The other day I bumped into him coming out of the bathroom. I think he must have been dying his hair again. He's been doing that a lot just lately. Can't seem to make up his mind on the colour, though. This time it was purple. He looked just like a half-eaten aubergine. Anyway, I asked him if he fancied a game of badminton. From the look he gave me you'd have thought I'd asked him to kiss our neighbour's dog's bottom! Have you seen our neighbour's dog?'

'Yes,' said Claire. 'It's a monstrosity, isn't it?'

'No, a Great Dane,' said Jason. 'Anyway, when I asked Dad about badminton, he looked daggers, then curled back his top lip and clawed the air, like this!'

Jason sucked in his cheeks and made his eyes bulge, then began swaying and doing some really impressive pretend clawing movements.

'Hmm – scary!' said Claire appreciatively.

'Then, on top of that,' continued Jason, 'he began hissing! Like this . . . psssss! haaasssss! pirsssaaaw! It went on for at least a minute. Then he just pulled his shawl over his head and galloped off down the landing.'

'Pulled his what over his head?'

'His shawl,' said Jason. 'He's taken to wearing this old black knitted one. It was one of my great-gran's. It's never off his back.'

'But Jason, your dad's a sharp-suited thirty-nine-year-old ex-professional footballer with a top of the range sports car and his own

67

chain of health food shops, keep fit clubs and laundrettes.'

'Not any more, he's not,' said Jason. 'He's a weirdo with a shawl. Sometimes he pulls it over his face and stares at you through the holes. It's really spooky! That's how he watches telly too. He reckons it stops the gamma rays from leaking out and eating his brain.'

'Cripes!' gasped Claire, unable to hide her horror. 'But what does your mum say about all this?'

'She says that it's total rubbish and that I mustn't take any notice,' said Jason. 'She thinks it's much better to hold a rook's wing in front of the set and chant magic spells backwards. That way you deflect the gamma rays and you stop the evil goblins who live beneath the satellite dish from knowing you're watching.'

'You what?' gasped Claire. 'So are you telling me that your mum has gone odd too?'

'Oh yes,' said Jason. 'She's not nearly as bad as Dad, though. At least she doesn't spend every other night licking the front drive and jumping off the garage roof.'

Chapter Seven
Vampires Impersonating People

Claire didn't manage to find out any more about Jason's parents' bizarre behaviour because at that moment a herd of wild, sweaty zoo animals thundered into the classroom, closely followed by an even wilder, sweatier zoo keeper.

When Mr Pither eventually got the animals seated, he said, 'OK everyone. As the season of spooky masks and stick-on scars is almost upon us, how about a lesson on fright-night fun and Hallowe'en high-jinks. Or would you prefer a Maths test?'

'Hallowe'eeen please, Mr Peeee!' yelled the whole class – apart from Jason, who was completely lost in thoughts of gravel-licking fathers and spell-chanting mothers, and Claire, who was wondering what the link was between the Turners' odd behaviour, and that of Grandpa Reg.

'OK!' howled Mr Pither. 'First we must go back to the days when you couldn't step out of your hovel without bumping into a hobgoblin, a flibbertigibbet or a – Ms McFlintlock!'

Mr Pither froze and stared at the ferocious figure that had just appeared at Class Five's doorway. It was Ms Shirley McFlintlock, Chumley Primary's hatchet-faced, hammer-headed, gravel-voiced, spiky-haired Head Teacher. Or Burly Shirley, as the children and teachers preferred to call her (but not to her face, of course).

'Mr Pither!' she snarled. 'I am about to bring some VIPs into your classroom. I will return in one minute. When I do, I expect you to behave as befits a teacher in my empire – I mean school. And your class to be scribbling away as though their lives depended on it.'

Then she charged off.

'Excuse me, Mr Pither,' said Darren Dobbs, who wasn't the brainiest boy in Class Five, but was certainly one of the most popular and also very keen to learn. 'What's a VIP? Some sort of snake?'

'No, Darren!' laughed Mr Pither. 'It stands for Very Important Person.'

Class Five grabbed their writing folders and soon were hard at work. Five seconds later, the classroom door flew open and Shirley marched in. As the class rose to its feet, Claire saw that the honoured guests were none other than Bruno and Hildegard Blodvat.

'Sit down please, children,' said Ms McFlintlock. She grinned creepily at the Blodvats and said, 'Dr Bruno and Madam Hildegard have come from a long way away to learn about life in Britain. In a moment, they will be speaking to Mr Pither. While they do I want you to all work as quietly as mice.'

Despite the fact that the class couldn't have been more fascinated by their strange visitors if Shirley had just led a pair of three-day-old Venusian cyber-puppies into the room, they did as they were told. However, try as they might, two of the students were unable to stop themselves sneaking fearful and disbelieving looks at the surprise guests. One, of course, was Claire. The other was Jason.

As Claire watched Shirley introducing the grinning Blodvats to her teacher, she thought, Mr Pither was wrong. No way is VIP short for Very Important Person. In their case, it stands for Vampires Impersonating People!

After curtseying a couple of times at

Hildegard, Mr Pither turned to Bruno, grasped his hand and said, 'Pleased to meet you. How do you do?'

'Too pleased I am!' replied Dr Bruno. 'How do you doodle?' Then he joined Hildegard, who had just spotted Claire, and was now waving and blowing her little kisses. Claire gave a limp wave back.

'Mr Pither,' said Shirley. 'Perhaps you will now spare our visitors a few minutes?'

'Yes, Ms McFlintlock,' said Mr Pither, and led the Blodvats to the quiet area.

As she did her best to get on with her work, Claire also tried her hardest to hear what the Blodvats were saying to Mr Pither. But as they were chatting quite quietly, this was impossible. All she knew was that Mr Pither looked confused and, at times, positively alarmed.

I can't sit here and do nothing, she thought. I've got to hear what they're saying. She stood up, wandered over to the library area, pretending to look for a book, until she was within earshot. Even then it was difficult to hear but she did manage to catch a few words. She definitely heard Bruno say 'Eck', 'navigable' and 'Harker'. A few seconds later she heard Hildegard say 'Whitby' and 'East Cliff'. She also thought she heard her say 'wolf gang'.

Just after that some sort of disagreement seemed to break out between Dr Blodvat and Mr Pither. Bruno's eyes went quite pink as he excitedly muttered the words 'remains' and 'comrades'. At which point, Mr Pither shook his head in exasperation, and said something that sounded like 'friction friction'. Trying to make sense of it all was incredibly frustrating.

'Young lady!' rasped a voice. 'Don't you think you've been long enough?'

'Yes, Ms McFlintlock!' said Claire. She quickly grabbed a book and returned to her seat.

Three minutes later, the Blodvats and Mr Pither finished their chat and came back, all looking like the best of friends. Claire was frantically trying to work out the answers to all the new questions whizzing around her brain. Like how the Blodvats had managed to get themselves invited to Chumley Primary? And what exactly had they been talking to Mr Pither about? And why had Jason been looking at Bruno and Hildegard with such a mixture of confusion and fearful familiarity? She was definitely going to speak to Jason again. The sooner the better!

Chapter Eight
Vampire Vigilantes

When Jason came out of school, Claire stopped him and said, 'Can I walk home with you? I want to ask you a couple of questions.'

'OK,' said Jason, as they set off down School Lane. 'Ask away!'

'Do you know the Blodvats?' said Claire. 'The weirdos Burly Shirley brought into class. You did a double take when you saw them – like you knew them?'

'Oh, them! Yes, I do. But that's not what my dad calls them.'

'Your dad knows them too?'

'Yes,' said Jason. 'That's why I recognized them. They really give me the creeps. They came to tea the other week. Spent the whole afternoon talking about how wonderful Chumley is. And showing us photos of their soppy kids.'

'How do they know your dad?' said Claire

'Some sort of business deal,' said Jason. 'He calls them the Directors. But whatever they were setting up fell through. It was around the time he began acting weird. Why? Do *you* know them?'

'Yes,' said Claire. 'And I'll tell you some things about them which might surprise you. But first, one more question.' Claire took a deep breath. 'Do you believe in vampires?'

Jason grinned and said, "Course not! They're pretend. Any sensible person knows all that climbing out of graves and blood drinking is twaddle!'

'I used to think that,' said Claire. 'But then I met Bruno and Hildegard. And now I've changed my mind.' And then she told him every single thing that had happened.

When she'd finished Jason said, 'Wow! That is amazing. Are you sure you're not making this up?'

'Not a single word,' said Claire. 'Promise! And you're the first person I've been able to tell everything to. It's all been fizzing around in my head for ages. Driving me crazy.'

'But why didn't you tell your parents? I'd tell mine about the stuff that's bothering me. Except . . . *they're* the problem.'

'It was a dead loss. Beastly Bruno and Horrendous Hildegard are their heroes!'

'But surely your folks should take some notice of you?'

'They ought to. But, well . . . I've got a really wild imagination and—'

'Yes,' said Jason. 'Dither's always going on about your brilliant stories.'

'I know,' said Claire. 'But sometimes I get *real* mixed with *make-believe*. Like with those cats. So now when I go to them with a story they don't believe me! But Jason, this time, I know I'm right. I just know the Blodvats are up to something. And I've a feeling that the something is big and dangerous, and it's connected with my Grandpa Reg and his blood pudding factory – and, from the sound of it, your dad and mum. But I'm sure it goes deeper and wider. And to be honest, being the only one who knows about it is like walking around with a really heavy weight attached to my head.'

'But you've told me now. Hasn't that helped?'

'Yes. I feel tons better.'

'Shouldn't that be tons lighter?'

Claire laughed and said, 'That too! But it doesn't solve the problem of what to do.'

Jason thought for a moment, then said, 'Look! I know I told you I didn't believe in vampires. But for some reason, I sort of believe this stuff you've told me about these Blodvats. And it's obvious what you have to do. Get proof. Something to show grown-ups. Like photos!'

'Jason!' cried Claire. 'I'm not dim – I thought of that yonks ago! But the idea of spying on those horrors terrifies me. They're so slippery and treacherous. There's no telling where they'll pop up next. I'd need eyes in the back of my head.'

'What if you had help? Wouldn't that make you feel better?'

'Of course. Fifty thousand times better!'

'So when do we start?'

'Jason – do you mean that?'

'Yes! Especially as it looks like these Blodvamps might well be the reason for my parents acting weird. Anyway, you haven't answered my question. When do we start?'

'Err, what about now?'

'OK. You've got yourself a partner! We'll be like one of those telly detective teams. You watch your back and I'll watch mine. Err, no – I'll watch your back and we'll watch theirs. I think? Anyway, we'll have to be really—'

'Watchful?' said Claire.

'No, sharper than that!' said Jason. 'A word Dither said. To do with being alert. It's on the tip of my tongue. What is it?'

'Spit!' said Claire.

'Ha blooming ha!' said Jason. 'Come on Claire – concentrate! It means always ready for trouble.'

'Ah!' said Claire. 'Vigilant!'

'Yes! Vigilant! That's what we'll be!'

'Hey! I've thought of something better! We could be vigilantes! So we're always alert but also protect everyone!'

'Brilliant!' said Jason, getting more excited by the moment. 'And I've just thought of a name for us.'

'So have I!'

And then, almost as if this moment was meant to happen, at exactly the same instant, the two of them said, 'We'll be Vampire Vigilantes!'

Chapter Nine

Talking Tactics

The newly-formed Vampire Vigilantes were so busy chatting about being vigilant that they walked straight past Jason's house. Then, realizing their mistake, they laughed and retraced their steps to 'Wembley', the swanky pad where Jason lived with his glamorous (but now, tragically weird) parents. As they stood by its enormous front gates Jason said, 'Claire, why don't you come in and talk tictacs? Sorry – tactics!'

Claire looked worried then said, 'I'd like to, but—'

'Ah!' said Jason, suddenly realizing what she was getting at. 'If you're worried about my folks going weird on you, forget it. They don't normally start until after seven. In fact, some nights it doesn't happen at all. You'll be fine. Just ring your mum and tell her you'll be late.'

'All right then,' said Claire. 'But I can't stay too long.'

When Jason's mum opened the front door she gave them both a big smile and said, 'Hi Jason! Hi Claire! Haven't seen you for a while. How are you doing?'

'Not bad at all thanks, Mum,' said Jason. 'And how are you?'

'I was talking to Claire,' said Mrs Turner.

'She's good, too!' said Jason. 'Can she come in? Mr Dither's given us a paired homework project on, err . . .'

'Local geology,' said Claire.

'Local geography,' said Jason.

'Geology,' said Claire.

'Yes,' said Jason. 'That too!'

'She seems incredibly normal,' said Claire, once they were in Jason's room.

'She is, mostly,' said Jason. 'It's just that they both seem to get taken over. Almost like some distant power zaps a remote.'

'Or controls them through hypnotism,' said Claire. 'Or telepathy.'

'What's tepalathy?' said Jason.

81

'Telepathy,' said Claire. 'It's having the power to send your thoughts to other people. And to read theirs. Just think what it would mean if Bruno or Hildegard could control your mum and dad or my Grandpa Reg by telepathy. It means that they could use them for their own evil ends. And if necessary, sacrifice them.'

Jason suddenly clapped his hand to his head and said, 'Hey! I've just remembered this film. It was called *Out For the Count*. This crusty old vampire was up in his castle in Tonsilveinia, controlling people by thinking things. He'd met this teacher when he was on holiday in England and he was making him do weird stuff that teachers don't normally do: smiling, being nice to pupils, that sort of thing. He'd even got him *eating flies!*'

When Jason said that, Claire remembered Grandpa Reg's insect collection. A cold chill ran up her spine, climbed on to her left shoulder, took a look around, decided it didn't like what it saw, then ran back down her spine again.

'Yes well,' she said, desperately trying to push all sorts of horrific thoughts from her head, 'We must be positive. Make plans.'

'Tell me,' said Jason. 'I'm all ears!'

'OK. For the next couple of days we can be

cool because Bruno and Hildegard are in London visiting Sir Norman Goreman.'

'Who's Gormless Sir Norman?'

'Some Government big cheese. While Bruno and Hildegard are hobnobbing with him you and me can work out—'

'Way to go, Claire!' yelled Jason, jumping up and punching the air. 'We'll use our gym – I'll take you up now. What do you think we should start on? Rowing machines? Joggers? Or shall we just pump some iron?'

Claire looked at him like he'd flipped, then said, 'What are you talking about?'

'Working out!' said Jason. 'It's what weedy guys do in films before they take on hard nuts. Get themselves in peak condition. Then beat their enemy's tripes out!' And he immediately began pummelling an imaginary enemy and shouting, 'Take that! And that! Yeah, don't like it when you get a taste of your own medicine, do you?'

'Jason!' cried Claire. 'Calm down! I was going to say you and I can work out a strategy.'

'Oh, right,' said Jason. 'Sorry, I just got a bit over-excited.'

'We'll have to get our act together quite quickly because I sort of know that the Blodvats are back next weekend. And I'm more or less sure they'll be up at Ravenscrag on Saturday afternoon.'

'What? The old ruin up above the Eck Estuary?'

'Yes,' said Claire. 'Something's arranged. I've no idea what but I'm certain it's very sinister.'

'You don't half know a lot about what they're up to,' said Jason, then he thought for a moment and said, 'Have you got pathetic-telly powers too?'

'No!' said Claire. 'I've got *this*!' She took a small book out of her pocket and waved it under Jason's nose.

'What's that?' he said.

'A key!'

'No it's not. It's a little red book.'

'Ha ha! Now, listen, cement brains. Do you remember I told you Bruno threw a fit when he bit that sarnie?'

''Course I do!' said Jason.

'Well,' said Claire. 'While he was rolling around, this must have fallen out of his pocket. I found it under our settee when I was helping tidy up afterwards. And I just know the stuff in it is incredibly important. Fortunately for us, Bruno doesn't seem to have twigged where he lost it. It's our lifeline, Jason. Best bit of luck I've had so far, apart from teaming up with you. But, there is one problem!'

'What's that then?'

'I can't read it!'

'Come off it! You're the best reader in class! Dither said so!'

'Yes! Maybe in English. But not in Tonsilveinian or whatever this lot's written in. Look!'

Claire flipped through the book so that Jason could see the blood-red scrawl that covered its pink pages. It was all in a foreign language, or possibly a code.

'Just a mo!' he said. 'If you can't read it, how do you know what you know?'

'Look at those doodles,' said Claire, continuing to flip through the book. 'They obviously mean something.' Then she pointed to a chart on the last page and said, 'And an idiot could work out what that is.'

'Phwoar yeah!' said Jason. 'You'd have to be a dimwit not to know!' Then he thought for a moment and said, 'Err, what is it?'

'A calendar!' said Claire. 'It's divided into twelve blocks for the months with regular spaces for weeks and days. By counting I've worked out this one must be this coming Saturday 8 October. See the red ring and the tiny doodle of an old-fashioned sailing ship. And just here, written in language I can understand, it says *Ravenscrag*. It's so tiny that I had to use Grandpa Reg's magnifying glass to read it. And next to that, in equally tiny writing, are the figures 1745.'

'Well in that case, forget it!' said Jason. '1745 was ages ago! Whoever it was will be long gone!'

'No, you dipstick!' said Claire. 'It's from the twenty-four hour clock!'

Then she noticed he was grinning. 'I do know really,' he said. 'It's quarter to six!'

'Yes. So you know what our first Blodwatch mission is?'

'Sure do! We're going up to Ravenscrag for some serious undercover surveillance!'

'Spot on!' said Claire. 'But before we do we've things to sort. Like keeping in touch. We need coded e-dresses. Maybe something to do with being Vampire Vigilantes!'

'Well, since Grandpa Reg was first to get nobbled, why not friendsofharker?'

'Excellent!' said Claire. 'Now, what do you know about Ravenscrag?'

'Nothing – but I'll research it. It might even give us some clues as to what the Blodvats have got planned.'

'Brilliant!' said Claire. 'And I'll get busy sorting our surveillance kit. We can keep each other up to speed with e-mails.'

'Sorted!' said Jason. 'No probs.'

NEW   FORWARD   ATTACHMENTS   SIGNATURE   OPTIONS   HELP

From claire.whimsy<friendsofharker.01@surfnet.com

To jason.turner<friendsofharker.02@surfnet.com

Date 5 October

Subject You Know What

Hi Jason
Big occasion! First friendsofharker
e-mail! Bad news, G.R. back in bed.
Dr G. re-examined him – says has
big bruise on btm! Asked Mum if she
knew how. Mum said no idea. But
I've a few! How's research?
P.S. Did you see TV news? Posho do
at 10 Downing Street. P.M., Sir
Norman Goreman and other big
cheeses. You know who slithering in
background!
Speak soon – Claire

email express

NEW   FORWARD   ATTACHMENTS   SIGNATURE   OPTIONS   HELP

From   jason.turner<friendsofharker.02@surfnet.com

To   claire.whimsy<friendsofharker.01@surfnet.com

Date   5 October

Subject   Ravenscrag – Spooky!

Hi Claire,
Sorry about G.R. My two aren't bad,
but Dad walking with limp! Maybe from
falling off garage roof? Here's
Ravenscrag stuff from tourism site.
PS Yes saw TV. Creeps!

. . . .

Ravenscrag
Location: Eck Estuary, North Sea
coast Nearest town: Chumley-by-Eck –
7 miles
Origins: Ravenscrag Abbey – built
AD 1222 – village grew round it:
Church, Ravenscrag Arms, 15
cottages.
Coastal Erosion: Village originally
2 miles from coast but by 1850s
churchyard and several cottages
right on cliff top.
Ravenscrag Disaster: 1863 Big storm
forty-feet high waves pounded
cliffs. At midnight, cliff collapsed
into sea, along with church 9
cottages and 15 villagers (drowned).

Open to visitors Mar–Sept.
Current situation: Village abandoned –
owned by Heritage Trust – cottages etc
Point of interest: Half churchyard now
in sea leaving graves exposed.
Skeletons poking out of cliff face:
Crumbling Corpse Cliff.

RAVENSCRAG
CLIFFS

ECK ESTUARY
NORTH SEA

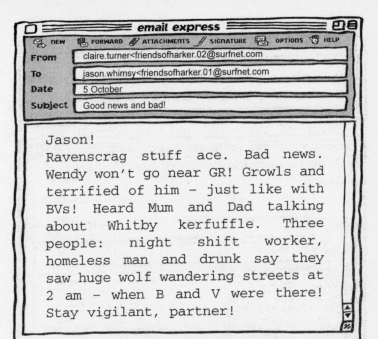

email express

NEW   FORWARD   ATTACHMENTS   SIGNATURE   OPTIONS   HELP

From	claire.turner<friendsofharker.02@surfnet.com
To	jason.whimsy<friendsofharker.01@surfnet.com
Date	5 October
Subject	Good news and bad!

Jason!
Ravenscrag stuff ace. Bad news.
Wendy won't go near GR! Growls and
terrified of him – just like with
BVs! Heard Mum and Dad talking
about Whitby kerfuffle. Three
people: night shift worker,
homeless man and drunk say they
saw huge wolf wandering streets at
2 am – when B and V were there!
Stay vigilant, partner!

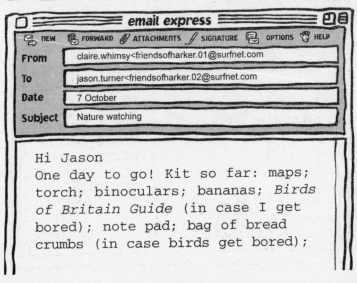

email express

NEW   FORWARD   ATTACHMENTS   SIGNATURE   OPTIONS   HELP

From	claire.whimsy<friendsofharker.01@surfnet.com
To	jason.turner<friendsofharker.02@surfnet.com
Date	7 October
Subject	Nature watching

Hi Jason
One day to go! Kit so far: maps;
torch; binoculars; bananas; *Birds
of Britain Guide* (in case I get
bored); note pad; bag of bread
crumbs (in case birds get bored);

puncture repair outfit; bottle of
pop; computer football game (in
case you get bored); camera (of
course!)C U - C PS Anything else?

email express

NEW   FORWARD   ATTACHMENTS   SIGNATURE   OPTIONS   HELP

From	jason.turner<friendsofharker.02@surfnet.com
To	claire.whimsy<friendsofharker.01@surfnet.com
Date	7 October
Subject	All at stake!

Hi Claire
Yes: what do we do if it gets physical?
Here's what vampire web pages say: How to
destroy a vampire:
1) Thrust a large wooden stake into the
vampire. Keep thrusting until it stops
moving.
2) Cut out the vampire's heart. Avoid
vampire blood splashes - could turn you
into vampire!
3) Burn the vampire's heart.
NB Never give up halfway through
destroying a vampire. Half-dead undeads
are worst sort. Scary, eh? But I
definitely think we should take a couple
of stonky great sharpened stakes. And a
box of matches! CU - J
PS Not keen on bananas. Got any pop tarts?
PPS What is anaemia? Loads in Chumley.

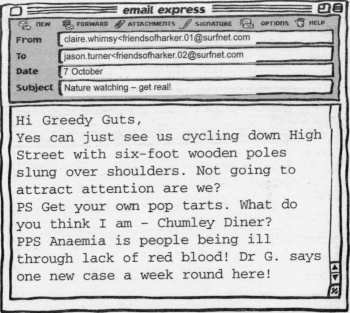

NEW   FORWARD   ATTACHMENTS   SIGNATURE   OPTIONS   HELP

From claire.whimsy<friendsofharker.01@surfnet.com

To jason.turner<friendsofharker.02@surfnet.com

Date 7 October

Subject Nature watching – get real!

Hi Greedy Guts,
Yes can just see us cycling down High
Street with six-foot wooden poles
slung over shoulders. Not going to
attract attention are we?
PS Get your own pop tarts. What do
you think I am – Chumley Diner?
PPS Anaemia is people being ill
through lack of red blood! Dr G. says
one new case a week round here!

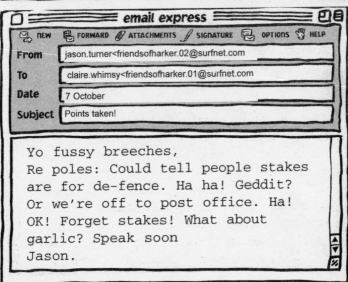

NEW   FORWARD   ATTACHMENTS   SIGNATURE   OPTIONS   HELP

From jason.turner<friendsofharker.02@surfnet.com

To claire.whimsy<friendsofharker.01@surfnet.com

Date 7 October

Subject Points taken!

Yo fussy breeches,
Re poles: Could tell people stakes
are for de-fence. Ha ha! Geddit?
Or we're off to post office. Ha!
OK! Forget stakes! What about
garlic? Speak soon
Jason.

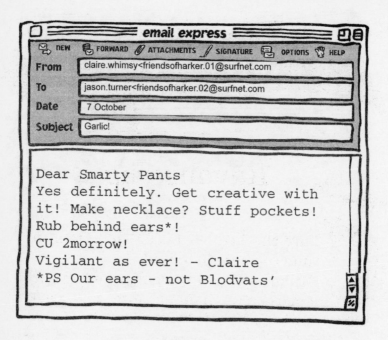

NEW FORWARD ATTACHMENTS SIGNATURE OPTIONS HELP

From claire.whimsy<friendsofharker.01@surfnet.com

To jason.turner<friendsofharker.02@surfnet.com

Date 7 October

Subject Garlic!

Dear Smarty Pants
Yes definitely. Get creative with
it! Make necklace? Stuff pockets!
Rub behind ears*!
CU 2morrow!
Vigilant as ever! – Claire
*PS Our ears - not Blodvats'

Chapter Ten

Ravenscrag

Claire checked her kit for the fifteenth time in as many minutes.

'Mum!' she said, stuffing a seventh (emergency) banana into her pack. 'Have we got any garlic?'

'What for?' said her mum.

'Err . . . to have with my snack!'

'With fruit?' said Mum.

'Perhaps not. Anyway, I'm off for a bike ride with Jason,' said Claire. 'Up to Ravenscrag to check out wildlife for our paired topic.'

'Well, you be careful,' said her mum.

'Why?' said Claire. 'Are paired topics dangerous?'

'You know what I mean,' said Mum. 'And make sure you start back before dark!'

'And if you're not, watch for werewolves!' said Dad. 'It's a full moon tonight.' Then he dropped on all fours and did his well-known (but completely pathetic) 'Lonesome Werewolf' impression. 'ARRROOOOOO!'

When Claire and Jason went into Legg's Greengrocers and asked for half a dozen bulbs of garlic, Mr Legg said, 'Crikey, you're the third today. I reckon it's down to that telly chef, ol' what's her face – Beth Burgignon. She did pigs' trotters smothered in crunchy garlic marmalade the other night. Can't abide 'em myself.. Just the sight of one makes me throw up!'

'What? Pigs' trotters?' said Jason.

'No, telly chefs!' said Mr Legg.

After an enjoyable ride only slightly spoilt by a couple of wrong turns and Jason falling off his bike when he demonstrated his pedalling-with-one-foot whilst steering-with-the-other technique, the Vigilantes finally reached the lane that led to Ravenscrag Village and saw a sign which said . . .

**ENGLISH NATIONAL
HERITAGE TRUST
WELCOME TO RAVENSCRAG –
CLOSED**

'Hmm, very friendly!' said Claire.

'So, what do we do with our bikes?' said Jason. 'Keep them with us or leave them in the pay and display car park?'

'You're kidding!' said Claire. 'If you did that you might as well put up a poster saying, "Dear Bruno and Hildy, we are keeping an eye on you. So, watch out! Love, Claire and Jason." Come on Jason, we're on an undercover mission. So let's act like it! We'll hide them in those bushes at the back of the ticket office.'

The Vigilantes stashed their bikes and had a shufty in the window of the visitors' centre where they admired the charming souvenir postcards of cottage-loads of villagers falling into the sea. Then, after noseying around the cottages and taking a squizz at the abbey, they finally wandered into the churchyard. Masses of it had toppled into the waves, but there was still about a quarter left with at least thirty graves. Some headstones were so near the cliff edge that they looked like they might crash into the water at any moment.

'Hey!' said Jason. 'This'll be where the skelebobs poke out of the cliff face. I'd like a look at them!'

'Tell you what!' said Claire. 'I'll hold your feet while you dangle. But if you slip out of your socks and nose-dive to the rocks, don't blame me!'

'I'll give it a miss,' said Jason. 'Let's just find a snooping spot!'

As they strolled around the headstones looking for a place to set up their spying post, Jason spotted a really worn and ancient stone, lying flat on the ground a few metres from the churchyard wall.

'This one looks prehistoric!' he said. 'And there's graffiti carved on it.'

Claire peered at the writing, then gasped, 'Wow, Jason! Look what it says: *Reg Harker— Dot Truscott, 23 August 1953*. Fancy that! My Grandpa Reg, a 1950s graffiti artist. I bet him and Granny Dot used to sit here gazing at the scenery.'

'The view is ace,' said Jason. 'It's a perfect spying post. We can lean against the headstones, then, if we do need to disappear, duck behind the churchyard wall!'

They quickly unloaded their packs and made themselves comfortable. 'So!' said Jason. 'What now?'

'We watch! We're Vigilantes!'

'But it's only four o'clock. There's nearly two hours to go!'

'I'd sooner be early than late. We'll play I-spy.'

'Err, crow?' said Jason. 'Canary? Cockatoo? Cuckoo? Oh, I give in!'

'It's a cormorant, stupid!' said Claire. 'Don't you know anything? Look, it's on that rock in the sea!'

'How was I to know?' said Jason. 'They all look like crows to me. Anyway, I'm fed up with I-spy. What time is it?'

'Half-past four.'

'So! What are we going to do next?'

'I know!' said Claire. 'We'll make ourselves a couple of those garlic clove necklaces I told you about!'

'Hmmm. Can't wait . . .'

'What do you think?' said Claire, as she held up her gorgeous garlic clove garland for inspection. 'An interesting and original work of art? A lovely item of jewellery that no self-respecting girl should be without?'

'Not really,' said Jason. 'More of a dog's dinner!'

'Yes!' said Claire. 'I agree. It looks stupid! And so does yours. But so what? If we're going to risk our necks we must protect them. And we don't have to have the grotty things on show. We'll slip them over our heads and hide them under our collars.'

'What time is it?' said Claire.

'Five-thirty-two,' said Jason. 'And no, I don't want another banana.'

'Don't be impatient,' said Claire. 'It's almost time. If we're right, something BIG is about to happen.'

'Yes, but what?'

'I dunno, but that's not the point. The important thing is to be prepared.'

'Right. Vigilant. Cool. Calm.'

'Courageous! Confident!' said Claire. 'Fearless! Her left knee began to twitch. 'Jason,' she said. 'Are you scared?'

'Me – scared?' said Jason. 'You must be kidding!' He put his hand on his heart. It was thumping like a turbo-charged dishwasher.

Suddenly they heard a noise. A slow, deliberate . . . scrunch . . . scrinch . . . scrunch . . . scronch.

'What was that!' muttered Claire.

'A baboon eating celery?' whispered Jason.

'Or an environmentalist ironing crisp packets?' muttered Claire.

But they both knew it was really footsteps on gravel.

And there it was again . . . Scrunch . . . scrinch . . . scrunch . . . scronch.

Claire's heart did a wild leap followed by two handstands and a backflip. Jason simply went hot, then cold, then hot again, then really, really cold.

'M-m-maybe it's a t-t-tourist looking for somewhere to b-b-be homesick?' he stammered.

'Or a sea bird practising the cha-cha?' murmured Claire.

'Or maybe it isn't,' they said together, then hurled themselves face down on the ground and began to commando wriggle towards the wall, keeping their faces pressed to the earth. Claire had never tasted soil before. It wasn't bad. Sort of nutty with a hint of lemon.

They reached the wall and peeped through the gaps in the stonework. An icy claw of fear instantly gripped Claire's tummy and squeezed it for all it was worth while a small pang of terror grabbed Jason's small intestine and whirled it gleefully around his head.

'Cripes!' he gasped. 'Look!'

A hooded figure was moving stealthily amongst the headstones. Crouched, ape-like, it scurried from grave to grave.

It had its back to them so it was impossible to make out who – or what – it might be. All they could see were dark clothes, that oh-so-sinister hood, and the odd jerky movements it made as it scampered around the cemetery.

'I think it's carrying something,' muttered Claire. 'But why does it keep putting them up to its eyes? I know! It's—'

'Binoculars!' whispered Jason.

'Yesss!' hissed Claire. 'It's watching for something. Some sort of rendezvous is going to take place! What time is it?'

They both looked at their watches. Five-thirty-six! Yes, the time was almost right. They looked up again, and their hearts sank. The hooded figure had vanished.

'Oh no!' whispered Jason. 'It could be

anywhere. Now we're in trouble. Let's go home!'

'Jason!' hissed Claire. 'Get a grip! Think of my grandpa. And your parents. Not to mention all the people who'll be incurably vamplified if we don't do our bit! Where's your spirit? We're going be brave! But cautious! So first, we'll—'

'Run away?' Jason said hopefully.

'No!' said Claire. 'We'll collect our bikes! That way, if things get really difficult, we can escape fast. But we aren't chickening out! Now, I'll count to three. Then we dash for that really enormous tombstone. We take cover behind it and get our breath back. Then do it all again! OK?'

'Yes,' said Jason. 'OK.'

'OK!' said Claire. 'Prepare to meet thy tomb! One two three. GO!'

They leapt to their feet. Sprinted through the grave stones. Got to the big tombstone. Dodged around it. And came face to face with the hooded prowler.

103

Chapter Eleven
Twitch! Twitch!

'Mr Pither!' gasped Claire and Jason together.

'CLAIRE! JASON!' gasped Mr Pither, fumbling with his binoculars' strap and getting into a right old dither.

Having expected to find themselves staring into the eyes of some drooling, foul-smelling, blood-sucking fiend who would instantly turn their necks into something that looked like it had fallen off Safebury's meat counter, Claire and Jason felt quite relieved to be staring into the slightly smeary spectacle lenses of a small, kind-looking man with a hairy chin. But at the same time they also felt incredibly disappointed. The last person they wanted to meet was their own class teacher.

They knew what he was doing here too.

When he wasn't being a teacher, Mr Pither was a bird watcher. Mr Pither was bird barmy!

'Oh dear!' said Mr Pither. 'You did give me a start! What are you doing here?'

'Working on a project,' said Jason. 'Our teacher told us to do it.'

'But I'm your teacher!' said Mr Pither.

'Oh yes,' said Jason, looking completely confused.

'Ignore him!' said Claire. 'It's a personal project. Hey, Mr Pither! I bet you're twitching.'

Mr Pither twitched a couple of times then said, 'Yes. I'd heard there were, err – a pair of Greater Speckled Rock Widgets up here! Some err – ornithologist friends of mine are doing a special study of them. They stop off here every autumn after spending the summer in Northern Melancholia where they eat nothing but crag worms and slurry spiders.'

'Uurgh gross!' exclaimed Jason. 'Can't your friends afford proper food?'

'I'm talking about the Rock Widgets,' said Mr Pither. 'And they really are amazing! After resting here they fly all the way to Mexico. Incredible, isn't it?'

'Astonishing,' said Claire. 'But how do your ornithologist friends know that's where they've gone?'

'They ring them,' said Mr Pither.

Claire was just about to ask Mr Pither if the Rock Widgets ever rang his friends, just for a change, and possibly to keep down the cost of international phone calls, when she glanced at her watch. It was exactly five-forty-five. Cripes! she thought. If we twitter any longer we'll miss whatever we're waiting for.

Preep preep! It was the sound of a mobile phone. Or possibly a small bird?

Mr Pither twitched and said, 'Oh! I wonder if that's them?'

'The Rock Widgets?' said Jason.

'No, my err . . . friends!' said Mr Pither. 'Now, where did I put it?'

Preep preep! went Mr Pither's mobile. It was getting louder! At first Mr Pither searched for his phone calmly but the less successful he was the more agitated he became. He was soon slapping himself all over. 'Oh, where did I put the bleeping thing?' said Mr Pither.

By now he was doing a demented dervish, tearing viciously at velcro, frantically unzipping zips and clutching desperately at various bits of his anatomy. And then, just when the Vigilantes were sure he would beat himself to death, or simply tear himself to shreds, he seemed to find what he was after.

'Ah, at last!' he said taking out a small black object and pressing it to his ear. 'Hellooo! Tony Pither speaking. How may I help?

PREEP PREEP . . . PREEP! went the phone.

Mr Pither's face fell. 'Oh fiddlesticks!' he cried, jumping up and down like a gibbon. 'It's not working. What will I do?'

Claire looked at Mr Pither's mobile, then said, 'Actually, I think you're talking into your TV remote control.'

Mr Pither stopped leaping, checked it, then giggled and said, 'Oh so I am!'

PREEEEEEEP PREEEP! went the phone. Suddenly there were two answering preeps. But sharper and shorter.

Preep preep!

'Ha!' said Mr Pither. 'Your mobile's ringing now.'

'Haven't got one,' said Claire.

'Nor me,' said Jason.

Preep preep!

Claire suddenly spied two brown, speckled birds sitting on a headstone. They were both looking at Mr Pither as though he were the most wonderful thing since sliced seedcake!

Preeeep! went the birds.

PREEEEEEEP! went Mr Pither's trouser leg.

'Look! Over there, Mr Pither!' cried Claire.

Still rummaging through his pockets Mr Pither followed the direction of her gaze.

'Well I never!' he cried. 'Greater Speckled Rock Widgets!'

'I think they like you Mr Pither,' said Jason. 'Or your mobile?'

Mr Pither didn't reply because he'd just found his phone. And he didn't waste a second answering it!

'Hellooo . . . Pither,' he shrieked. Then he paused and said, 'Yes! Of course! I'm on my way . . . now!' He looked at Jason and Claire and said, 'It's my friends! I must fly!' and he went scampering off over the heath.

'Oh dear!' said Claire. 'He forgot to tell his friends about the Rock Widgets . . .'

Chapter Twelve
The Worm

'Hmmmph!' grumbled Jason. 'So much for being up an' at 'em rootin' tootin' not let anything faze us Vampire Vigibloomin'-lantes! Here we are, all ready to zap the forces of evil, and what happens? Our bird-brained teacher turns up and starts twittering on about Rock Fidgets. Then, just when something BIG is supposed to happen, he does a war dance with his mobile! So that's that! Looks like we've blown it.'

He paused and sighed, then tapped his watch and said, 'Anyway, I don't think there was even going to be a BIG whatever. Look, it's five past six – it'll soon be dark, and nothing has happened. To be honest, I think we've probably got it all wrong. Maybe the Blodvats aren't vampires. And your grandpa and my folks have gone senile.'

'Now listen, Jason, We're definitely not giving up. For starters you just mentioned something really important. Mr Pither's mobile rang at the exact moment something BIG was due to happen. In other words, five-forty-five! Now, that could be coincidence. Or it could be . . .'

Suddenly Jason beamed at Claire, then said, 'That he was involved too?'

'Yes. I'm more certain by the minute!'

Jason nodded, then said, 'He did have that chat with the Blodvats, didn't he? And they definitely seemed to want something from him.'

'Without a doubt,' said Claire. 'And the other thing that's really weird are those Rock Widgets. They're mega-rare and he's a twitcher – and twitchers are fanatical about keeping mates up to speed on everything! So why didn't he immediately tell his twitcher friends on the phone about the Rock Widgets? If it *was* his twitcher friends.'

'Ah yes! But how does all this affect us right now?'

'I'm not sure,' said Claire. 'I think we've just got to collect our stuff, go home, and re-think. I'm almost certain nothing else will happen today.'

'Hey Claire!' said Jason. 'Did you see that?'

'No,' said Claire. 'What?'

'The binoculars! They just toppled over. All on their own! And hey – look at that!'

He pointed to her camera. It was shaking, then it tipped over. All at once they realized what was happening.

'It's the ground!' Claire gasped. 'It's trembling! Like a mini-earthquake!'

Suddenly Jason relaxed, then smiled and said, 'No sweat! It's a mole!'

'If it is, it's a big one,' said Claire. 'Just look now!'

Jason suddenly jumped back. 'Claire!' he yelled. 'Get back! Look at that!'

Claire followed his gaze. There was a grotesque pink object thrusting out of the shaking earth.

'Uuurgh!' she gasped. 'What is it?'

'S–s–some sort of worm, I think!' gasped Jason. 'But it's just so massive!'

It was. As he'd been speaking at least another eight centimetres of the repulsive thing had thrust upwards. It was now waving and thrashing wildly. And at that moment it was plain to see that it wasn't a worm at all!

'Claire,' groaned Jason. 'It's not a worm! It's not a worm! It's a – tongue!'

But Claire wasn't looking. Or listening. While she'd been watching the heaving ground, completely unbeknownst to her, a long, claw-like object had thrust through the earth by her foot. It was a finger! Soon it was joined by more fingers, some knuckles, and finally a wrist.

She looked down, just in time to see this utterly horrifying hand break free of the ground, then claw at the air next to her leg. If she'd moved a fraction of a second earlier she might have avoided its grip. But she didn't. So all she could do was watch helplessly as those terrible talons slowly and cruelly encircled her ankle. A moment later, she felt their cold clamminess spreading over her skin, and, as those horrid fingernails pressed into her flesh, she began to scream – and scream.

Chapter
Thirteen

Skrungy

'AARGH! Aaargh!' yelled Claire. 'It's got me! It's got me!'

Horror-stricken, she stared down at the mud-encrusted claw that held her ankle in its terrible vice-like grip. It had now pushed so far out of the ground that she could also see the lower half of a very hairy arm. She was desperate for Jason to come to her rescue. But he was still completely mesmerized by the horrendous, spongy, pink tongue which was lashing furiously like an angry pink serpent. But then, as she screamed an extra loud and ear-splitting scream, her predicament finally seemed to dawn on him and he sprang to her rescue.

'Get it off me, Jason!' Claire screeched. 'Pleeeeeeeeeeeeease!'

Jason fell to his knees, seized the wrist

and yelled, 'Leave her alone! Let go!'

'Jason!' screamed Claire. 'Don't shout at it. Just get it off!'

Jason instantly put all his energy into trying to bend back the huge fingers that encircled Claire's ankle. He might as well have tried to bend gold bars. 'It's no good!' he gasped. 'They won't budge!'

'Well bite it!' screamed Claire. 'Bite it, you daft wimp! Before it's too late!'

Jason gave Claire a slightly hurt look, stared at the hand for a moment, then sank his teeth into it, shaking his head and making ferocious 'GRRRRR! GRRRRR!' noises.

'Atta boy!' yelled Claire. 'That's more like it! Chew it up, Fido!'

The fingers suddenly sprang open like a trap and the ground around them juddered and heaved more violently than ever. As Jason shot to his feet, Claire leapt clear of the clawing fingers. Then, still trembling all over, she said, 'Thanks! You saved my skin.'

'No problem,' said Jason. 'I was just doing my bit – I mean bite.'

Claire smiled, then said, 'OK! We need to act fast! Let's grab our stuff and put a safe distance between ourselves and *that*! Before any more appears.'

Almost the whole arm was out of the

ground now, thrashing around blindly, desperately seeking something else to ensnare in its terrible grip! Keeping a wary eye on the menacing mitt, they hurriedly stuffed their belongings into their packs.

'Right!' said Jason. 'Let's go! We won't stop until we're back in Chumley!'

Claire looked at him as if he'd taken leave of his senses. 'What do you mean?' she said. 'I want to see what happens next!'

But then she screamed and pointed to a patch of turf next to Jason's foot. In the few seconds they'd been talking another hand had pushed through the earth. And this one was thrusting upwards far more rapidly than the first. The hand and the lower arm were already out! They didn't wait for the elbow! Grabbing their packs they sprinted across the graveyard towards the abbey like their feet were on fire. The moment they reached it, they dashed through an archway, but were instantly brought to an abrupt halt, barred by a large and ancient wooden door.

'Rats!' said Jason. 'What are we gonna do now?'

'Kick it!' said Claire. 'It doesn't look strong. See! The wood's rotted and the padlock and hinges are manky and rusted!'

'But – but – that would be vandalism!'

116

said Jason. 'And this notice says "Only to be used in emergency".'

'Jason!' said Claire. 'This is an emergency! Quite soon the owner of those hands is going to be up and about. We need a hiding place – fast!'

'So, what are we waiting for?' said Jason, and with that they both gave the door such an almighty kick that it groaned once, creaked twice, then fell off its hinges, hitting the floor with an enormous bang. Behind it was another archway, and beyond that a spiral stone staircase.

'Great!' said Claire. 'Those stairs must lead up the abbey tower. Let's go!'

They dashed through the next archway then whirled dizzily up the crumbling spiral steps. After scrambling up at least a hundred, they reached a landing and collapsed in two exhausted, throbbing heaps. When they'd got their breath back, they dragged themselves to an opening in the damp, musty-smelling stonework. Below them, not too far away, the hairy arms and the horrendous tongue were still waving frantically, like a trio of monstrous mutant plants from some nightmare garden centre.

'What a sight,' said Claire. 'I feel quite yukky.'

'Me too,' said Jason. 'It's gruesome!'

'But perfect for our first snap,' said Claire. 'Pass the camera!'

'Camera?' said Jason.

'Yes!' said Claire. 'For the snap! You picked it up, didn't you?'

'Err, no,' said Jason. 'I thought you did.'

'You're kidding?' groaned Claire. Then she looked at Jason's miserable face, saw he wasn't and said, 'So, where is it?'

'Down there,' said Jason, pointing to the turf they'd just fled.

Claire looked and there it was – next to

the arms! She was just thinking about dashing back to retrieve it, or maybe pushing Jason out of the window, when the arms suddenly froze in midair. A split second later they exploded into hyper-action and began digging like a couple of rocket-driven JCBs. Soon, clods of earth were flying in all directions.

'Wow!' gasped Claire. 'Forget the camera! Whoever's down there is definitely getting ready for their evening out! What time is it?'

Jason looked at his watch and said, 'Six-thirty!'

'Time for things unearthly to be up and sucking!' said Claire. 'Well, we've no camera but at least we can watch the show by moonlight! Look at that!'

The hands had completely uncovered what looked like a large wooden plank and were desperately trying to get a grip on it.

'Cripes!' exclaimed Jason. 'It's a coffin lid!' Claire suddenly remembered the luggage in the Blodmobile.

The hands raised the lid slightly, then hurled it straight into the air. It came back down with a *clunk!* followed by what sounded like a groan.

'No technique, some people,' said Claire.

Once more the hands seized the lid and hurled it skywards. Down it came again with an enormous *thud!* This time the Vigilantes definitely heard a cry of pain. The hands had seized the lid yet again, but this time, instead of hurling it upwards, they threw it at an angle, so that it landed a couple of metres away.

'Brilliant!' said Jason. 'Third time lucky!'

With their hearts thudding so violently they could probably be heard in Chumley, the Vigilantes craned their necks, desperate to see what dreadful thing had finally uncovered itself. Despite the fact that a cloud passed over the moon at that very moment they could clearly make out that a very large hole had now appeared in the turf. It contained something big and vaguely human-shaped, dressed entirely in black. It twitched, then got to its feet. After sniffing the air, it clambered out of the hole . . .

Chapter Fourteen
Give Blood Now!

t's doing *exercises*!' said Jason, watching as the big and vaguely human-shaped thing did a few knee bends, followed by some toe touching.

'So would you,' said Claire, 'if you'd been cramped up in a box for ages!'

'I suppose so,' said Jason, then he grinned and said, 'Maybe its legs are dead, ha!'

'More like *undead*!' said Claire.

All of a sudden the something exploded into a furious burst of jogging on-the-spot, drew itself to its full height – at least seven feet – then threw back its head and let out an horrendous YOWL. A sound so terrifying that it sent the ravens screaming from the abbey. The noise of the birds suddenly caught the creature's attention and it turned and looked up at the tower. And as it did, the moon came

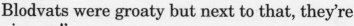

from behind the cloud, giving the Vigilantes their first clear view of its face.

'Uuurgh!' groaned Jason. 'Skrungeee!'

'Not half!' said Claire. 'I thought the Blodvats were groaty but next to that, they're pin-ups!'

Cold blue moonlight was now flooding the churchyard so they were clearly able to see the thing's semi-luminous, sickly green skin, its spiky, white hair and the red, pupils that glowed so intensely from its filthy yellow eyeballs. Then, just to complete the picture, it yawned, giving them a superb view of its filthy, jagged fangs. They were yellow, just like its eyes, and exactly the same shape as the thorns on Grandpa Reg's prize roses – only six times bigger.

'Definitely a vampire!' said Jason.

'Undoubtedly!' said Claire. 'He may never win a Gorgeous Ghoul contest but I'd still like a snap. If only we had my camera! I wonder if we could nip and nab it while he's yowling?'

Just as they were trying work out how they might retrieve the camera without getting mangled, fangled, or seriously strangled, Skrungy unexpectedly climbed back into his hole.

'Hey!' said Jason. 'He's gone back to bed. Wonder what for?'

'Beauty sleep,' said Claire.

She was wrong. A second later he climbed out. And when he did they could hardly believe their eyes!

'Jason?' said Claire. 'Is he wearing what I think he's wearing?'

'Well!' said Jason. 'If you mean, is that seven foot tall, yellow-fanged horrendosity down there wearing a bright green baseball cap, yes, he is. And, in case you hadn't noticed, he's also carrying a red and yellow skateboard!'

'Yes!' said Claire. 'I was just going to ask you about that. Jason, why ever would a vampire be carrying a skateboard?'

'Search me,' said Jason. 'This whole thing just gets weirder by the minute!'

'It just got scarier too,' said Claire. 'He's heading our way!'

With his skateboard tucked under his arm the grotesque graveyard guzzler was lumbering towards the tower.

'Oh no!' gasped Jason. 'Perhaps he's spotted us. If he traps us here, we're done for. Apart from the stairs, there's no way out! We'll be at his mercy!'

Skrungy had now reached the tower and was loitering by the archway directly below them. They could clearly read the reassuring words: GIVE BLOOD – NOW! written across his green baseball cap in large red letters!

'Yipes!' whispered Claire. 'I've seen those before! They were giving them out from the Eck Valley Mobile Blood Donors' van last week. So where's he got it from?'

'Haven't the faintest!' whispered Jason. 'But I do know something. At this moment he's at our mercy! All we have to do is drop a heavy object on him. Then SPLATT! KERDUMMMPH! BINGO! One zapped vamp! Brilliant – or what?'

'Brilliant!' said Claire. 'But there is one snag. I don't know about you, but I completely forgot to pack the huge four-ton boulder I keep under my bed and have been saving for just such an emergency as this! Come on Jason – get real! Exactly what sort of heavy weight are you thinking of?'

'Oh I dunno,' said Jason, looking around desperately but only seeing their backpacks.

'Surely there must be something we can bomb him with. Hey! What about your bananas? Even light objects can be deadly if you drop them from high enough.'

'Jason!' said Claire. 'We're trying to knock him senseless, not turn him into a fruit salad!'

'But there's got to be something!' said Jason. 'Once he starts up the steps our chance will be gone. How about your binoculars?'

'No way!' said Claire. 'Mum gave them to dad for his fortieth. He'd go scranny! Anyway, we may need them. Skrungy's wandering off.'

'Hey, he is too!' said Jason. 'You know what this means, don't you?'

'What?' said Claire.

'It means we won't have to splatter him after all!'

'Jason! How did you work that out? You must have the brain of a genius.'

'I have! But he wants it back next Tuesday.'

They both laughed, then sighed with relief as 'Skrungy' ambled on to the car park.

'Look!' said Jason. 'He's stopped at the 'Pay and Display' machine. Why do you think he's doing that, Claire?'

'I dunno,' said Claire. 'Perhaps he actually enjoys sticking his tongue in the coin slot? Hey! What's he doing now? Surely he's not going to—?'

'He is! He is!' gasped Jason, hardly able to contain his excitement.

As the Vigilantes watched in open-mouthed amazement, Skrungy dropped his skateboard on to the tarmac and hopped on as skilfully and nimbly as a junior Olympic gymnast. A moment later, he began to perform the most spectacular series of skateboard manoeuvres they'd ever seen. They watched in awe as he pushed off with a graceful Foot-Flick, slid expertly into a brilliant Backside Boardslide, performed a perfect Frontside Flip, followed it with a superb Triple Ollie, then finished with a brilliant Fakie Pivot Grind, all spectacularly accompanied by a chorus of blood-curdling yowls.

'Wow!' gasped Jason. 'And I thought Darren was an ace skateboarder! Yeah – way to go Skrungy! Way to go!'

'Jason,' said Claire. 'Stop it!'

'Stop what?' said Jason.

'That!' said Claire, pointing down at his hands.

Jason looked down at his hands. He was clapping!

'Oh! Yes – right!' he said sheepishly. 'Sorry

about that!' Then he thrust his hands into his pockets.

'Jason,' said Claire. 'It may have escaped your notice but that thing down there is not your mate. It's a recently risen vampire who would sink its fangs into your tender ten-year-old neck as easy as wink!'

'Or drink?' said Jason. 'Yes, I'll calm down.' Then he looked down at Skrungy and said, 'Anyway, what's he up to now!?'

The skateboarding bloodsucker had wandered a bit further away, obviously preparing himself for yet another sequence of breathtaking stunts.

'This is our chance,' said Claire. 'While he's busy Twistflipping we'll nab my camera!'

Jason looked worried, then said, 'Are you sure it's safe?'

'Of course not,' said Claire. 'But that isn't the point. We're here to get evidence. To be ruthless! Fearless!'

'Sensible?' said Jason. Then he saw the determined look on his fellow Vigilante's face and said, 'Yes, OK. But we better be quick!'

The Vigilantes scooted down the spiral staircase faster than soap slithering down a wet helter skelter. However, they were only halfway out of the arched porchway when the sound of a familiar voice caused an icy chill, two stabs of terror and seven thousand shivers of naked fear to race madly up and down their spines!

'Yoo hoo!' cried the voice. 'I'm heeeeyer!'

They both ducked back inside. After waiting a moment, they risked a cautious peep out, scanning the moonlit graveyard, but saw no one. The voice didn't appear to have an owner.

'That's weird,' whispered Claire. 'If I didn't know better I'd have said that was the sea calling.'

And then they heard it a second time!

'Yoo hoo!' it cried. 'I'm over heeeyer!'

But, apart from the wildly skateboarding Skrungy, there still didn't seem to be anyone else around.

And then they saw two tiny hands appear over the cliff edge. They were followed by a tiny head.

'Vladimir!' said Hildegard Blodvat. 'Vot effer are you up to?'

**To be continued in
VAMPIRE VIGILANTES 2:
NIGHTMARE ON ECK STREET**